"I don't think I've met your date, Nick,"

Stephanie said with a smile.

"Nikki, meet Stephanie. Stephanie, this is my favorite niece, Nikki."

The four-year-old dimpled. "I think you're pretty," she said to Stephanie. "Uncle Nick doesn't have a girlfriend. I've got a boyfriend," she confided. "His name is Zach. Do you have one?"

Stephanie felt a blush warm her ears. Was everyone curious about her social life? "Not at present."

"Do you have a little girl?" she continued.

"No, I have a son. But he's a little old for you."

As they chatted, Stephanie looked around the crowded diner. Heat seeped into her cheeks. In a small town, memories were long. The townsfolk would recall that she and Nick had once been inseparable. She'd thought they would be a family....

But now she knew that could never be.

Or could it?

Dear Reader,

This month, Silhouette Romance has six irresistible, emotional and heartwarming love stories for you, starting with our FABULOUS FATHERS title, *Wanted: One Son* by Laurie Paige. Deputy sheriff Nick Dorelli had watched the woman he loved marry another and have that man's child. But now, mother and child need Nick. Next is *The Bride Price* by bestselling author Suzanne Carey. Kyra Martin has fuzzy memories of having just married her Navajo ex-fiancé in a traditional wedding ceremony. And when she discovers she's expecting his child, she knows her dream was not only real…but had mysteriously come true! We also have two not-to-be missed new miniseries starting this month, beginning with *Miss Prim's Untamable Cowboy,* book 1 of THE BRUBAKER BRIDES by Carolyn Zane. A prim image consultant tries to tame a very masculine working-class wrangler into the true Texas millionaire tycoon he really is. Good luck, Miss Prim!

In *Only Bachelors Need Apply* by Charlotte Maclay, a man-shy woman's handsome new neighbor has some secrets that will make her the happiest woman in the world, and in *The Tycoon and the Townie* by Elizabeth Lane, a struggling waitress from the wrong side of the tracks is romanced by a handsome, wealthy bachelor. Finally, our other new miniseries, ROYAL WEDDINGS by Lisa Kaye Laurel. The lovely caretaker of a royal castle finds herself a prince's bride-to-be during a ball…with high hopes for happily ever after in *The Prince's Bride.*

I hope you enjoy all six of Silhouette Romance's terrific novels this month…and every month.

Regards,

Melissa Senate,
Senior Editor

Please address questions and book requests to:
Silhouette Reader Service
U.S.: 3010 Walden Ave., P.O. Box 1325, Buffalo, NY 14269
Canadian: P.O. Box 609, Fort Erie, Ont. L2A 5X3

WANTED: ONE SON

Laurie Paige

Silhouette
R O M A N C E™
Published by Silhouette Books
America's Publisher of Contemporary Romance

SILHOUETTE BOOKS

ISBN 0-373-19246-0

WANTED: ONE SON

Printed in U.S.A.

Books by Laurie Paige

LAURIE PAIGE

was recently presented with the *Affaire de Coeur* Readers' Choice Silver Pen Award for Favorite Contemporary Author. In addition, she was a 1994 Romance Writers of America (RITA) finalist for Best Traditional Romance for her book, *Sally's Beau*. She reports romance is blooming in her part of Northern California. With the birth of her second grandson, she finds herself madly in love with three wonderful males—"all hero material." So far, her husband hasn't complained about the other men in her life.

Dear Doogie,

Sometimes, when a fellow is hurting, he does a stupid thing. I know. I've been there. Once in anger and hurt, I reacted before thinking, then pride and stubbornness kept me from admitting I just might have been wrong. That cost me the future—and the family—I thought I'd have.

Well, a man makes his choices.

The only problem then is you have to live with them. Make sure yours are the ones you truly want.

Your dad was lucky in having a son like you. I thought so the first time I met you, and I still do. You have the makings of a fine man. I know I'd be proud to call you "son."

Your mom's a little uptight about things right now, but be honest with her, and you two will work it out. For one thing—she loves you. Don't ever forget that. I did once, and it cost me. That's neither here nor there. Just remember, you can talk to me anytime. I'll be here.

Love,

Nick

Chapter One

Nicholas Dorelli shifted restlessly from his left foot to his right, but his attention didn't wander. He watched his quarry with the expertise honed by ten years on the job. As a senior deputy sheriff and special investigator in Colorado, he was there on business. Stephanie Bolt was that business.

He tongued a toothpick from the right side of his mouth to the left. With a quick jab of his fingers, he shoved the annoying wing of hair that arced over his forehead to the side, where it stayed momentarily before returning to its natural position. He settled his hat with a firm tug over the stubborn cowlick and wished he was anyplace but here.

"Here" was the public park. Stephanie was sitting on a bench gazing at the mountains that surrounded the small town high in the Rockies.

Her short brown hair glowed with honey highlights in the June sun. She caught the strands blowing across her face and hooked them behind her ear. Her wedding band reflected the warm noon light, winking at him across the well-tended lawn of the park as if laughing at a private joke.

The joke was on him. Once she'd been his girl. Until he'd found her in the arms of another man.

For three months that fateful winter while he'd been away at college, he'd refused to believe the friends who reported Steph was seeing another man, not even when his own brother had confirmed it. He'd come home on spring break, determined to find out the truth. He had.

Steph, the woman he'd trusted. Steph, who'd clung to him for comfort at her father's funeral only three months before. Steph, who'd been his first love, had sat on her front porch and let another man hold and caress her....

After all these years, that bitter betrayal still lingered like a burr under his hide.

So did the hunger. It made him angry, this need that wouldn't go away. With it came a sense of things unfinished, the tattered ends of emotions left over from those days when he'd thought the world was his for the taking.

He shook his head slightly, as if he could cast off the past and the feelings associated with it. It had been a mistake to return home when he finished at the police academy. Having graduated at the top of his class, he'd been offered a job with the FBI in Virginia, a long way from here and from memories....

He watched as she plucked a blade of grass, and he wondered what she'd felt for her husband. She'd certainly played the faithful and dutiful widow in the two years since Clay's death. Too bad she hadn't been as faithful as a lover.... He cursed silently.

When she stood, the breeze pressed her silk shirt against her breasts. Her skirt folded between her thighs. He clenched his teeth. The toothpick snapped in half.

With a grimace he dropped the two pieces into the pine needles and shoved himself off the wrought iron fence. Stephanie was heading his way.

He knew the moment she spotted him.

She stopped and watched him. Her eyes, blue as the noontime sky, seemed to become even deeper in tone. She opened the gate, stepped out, then closed it behind her, her movements precise as she made sure the latch clicked into place.

"Nick," she said.

Not exactly a fond greeting for the man who had once been the love of her life, or so she'd claimed. They'd gone steady during their last year of high school and first year of college.

He cursed silently and nodded his head. "Stephanie."

He noticed the faint perpetual frown she'd worn for two years. He observed the tiny, perfectly round mole one inch from the corner of her mouth on the left, a place just made for kissing...before a man moved on to the lush fullness of her lips.

She was a woman to make a man dream. Full breasts. Slender waist. Rounded hips. Shapely legs. At five-nine, she was a good height for him. In heels, she'd fit his six-one frame perfectly. Once, they'd danced the night away, locked together so tightly he couldn't tell where he ended and she began.

She'd seldom worn heels during her marriage. That would have put her taller than Clay.

A knot formed in his throat, startling him with the unexpected emotion. Clay had been his mentor on the force, taking him on as his partner when Nick was a rookie, as green as a spring leaf on a cottonwood. It had been difficult, but he'd learned to admire the seasoned officer who was eight years his senior and husband to the woman he had thought to wed.

"What brings you here?" she asked, her eyes wary.

He'd put that wariness there. Last Christmas, after a cup of hot buttered rum, he'd kissed her at the mayor's annual party.

The mayor's wife had hung mistletoe over every door. He'd resisted temptation for an hour. When he'd run into Stephanie in the kitchen doorway, the mistletoe had been in place, they'd been alone for a minute and he'd given in to the passion that had erupted abruptly, catching him off guard.

So sue him.

"Doogie," he answered her question.

Surprise flew over her face, then she became wary again. "Doogie?" She sounded suspicious, as if she thought he might be lying for his own nefarious purposes.

"Yeah." He hesitated to disclose his news.

"If he were hurt, I assume you'd tell me right off."

"Of course."

"So he must be in trouble." She hooked the hair behind her ear with an impatient gesture. Her fingers trembled slightly. "What'd he do this time?"

"This time?"

"Last week he got in a fight with Clyde Marlow."

"Clyde's his best friend," Nick said, filing the information away. It tied in with his reason for being there.

"Not anymore."

Nick shoved his hands into his back pockets and considered. "Sounds like the boy needs help."

Her shoulders stiffened. Hostility boiled between them, distorting the air like summer heat on asphalt. It was a defensive reaction on her part, he reminded himself. On his part, neither anger nor any other emotion had a place in his dealings with her. She was simply the parent with a kid in trouble.

"Doogie…Douglas is fine. He's just…" Her voice trailed off, and she looked uncertain.

"Going through a phase?" He ended it for her.

"Yes. All boys get up to mischief. What has he done now? Another fight?" She almost looked hopeful.

"Shoplifting." The word came out harder than he meant it to do, but there was no way to pretty it up.

Her shoulders sagged. She closed her eyes for a second while she dragged in a shaky breath. Her skin, usually a smooth, healthy pink, mottled.

Nick took a step forward, his hands going out, his arms opening instinctively before he caught himself. He tucked his hands into his back pockets again, where they'd be safe, and backed up a step.

She opened her eyes, and he saw the heat in the usually cool depths. He steeled himself. People always took their anger out on cops. The Bad News Boys, as the sheriff labeled them in his jocular moments.

"Where? What?" she asked.

"Video, over at Joe Moss's."

"A video," she echoed. "Why? Why would he do something like that?"

He shrugged. "Kids."

"Is he in…at the jail?"

"No. I, umm…Joe decided not to prosecute."

"You talked him out of it. I…thank you. Where's Douglas? Did you take him back to the store?"

"Yeah." He knew the boy stayed in town on Saturdays, hanging around the clothing and accessories boutique that Stephanie successfully owned and managed with the mayor's wife. The kid ran errands for some of the merchants or went to a movie. It could be a lonely life for a twelve-year-old.

Stephanie was pretty strict about who her son was with and where he went. Since Clay's death she was even more so. That's what Nick had heard. He didn't see her much. He didn't want to. Steph was a part of his past that he'd never come to grips with. The fact that she still had the power to bother him made him angry, but that's the way it was.

Okay, he could handle it.

"Did you drive up?" She looked around for his cruiser, a four-wheel-drive utility truck.

"Yeah. Down here under the trees."

She'd walked the half mile from the Glass Slipper Boutique to the isolated park on a rise at the edge of town, a thing she often did during her brief periods of freedom. He shortened his steps to her pace and guided her down the sidewalk and around the corner.

The cruiser was parked in the shade of some ancient cottonwoods. A creek ran along the road and under a thirty-foot bridge nearby. The spot was pretty, romantic even. There was a nice grassy area for a picnic. Bittercress bobbed and nodded in shades of pink, white and yellow.

Not that *she* took the time to notice.

Without waiting for him, she wrenched open the truck door and attempted to climb inside. Her skirt was too narrow. She hiked it midway to her thigh, but still couldn't manage. He hooked his hands on each side of her waist and lifted her.

He held himself in check as her perfume wafted around them, brought out by the warmth of the sun and the exertion of the fast walk. He was aware of the hitch in her breathing and swallowed a groan that crowded his throat.

She fell back against him, and he realized he'd taken

her by surprise. Strength flowed into him in a tidal wave of adrenaline and hunger. She wasn't a featherweight, but neither did she feel heavy. In fact, she felt wonderful in his arms, but then, she'd always felt perfect to him during those long-ago days.

"You can put me down now."

Her voice came from far away, barely audible over the roar of the blood pulsing through his ears.

"Nick! Nicholas! Put me down."

The sharp panic that underlined the command jerked him back from the edge of control. He released her and slammed the door.

Stalking behind the truck, he paused and swiped a hand over his forehead where sweat had gathered in a fine-beaded sheen. He caught sight of himself in the tinted rear window.

Picture of a haunted man.

He yanked his sunglasses from his shirt pocket and jammed them on his nose. There, he thought, that at least hid the treachery of raging lust from her view. The anger surged anew. He didn't want to be susceptible to Stephanie. He forced himself to calmly walk to the driver's door and climb in.

When the engine was purring, he flicked the fan to high. Cool air swirled around them, drowning out the need to talk as he eased into gear and headed for the heart of the town nestled in the foothills of the Rockies, an hour out from Denver.

Stephanie hopped out of the truck before Nick had a chance to come around and lift her down. His eyes, dark as bitter chocolate when he removed his sunglasses, bored into hers.

"Thanks for the ride. And for taking care of Doogie."

"It was nothing."

She nodded, closed the door and dashed across the parking lot to the boutique before he could say more. One thing she didn't need was advice from a thirty-four-year-old bachelor on how to raise her son. She was only three months younger than Nick Dorelli. She and Doogie were doing fine, just fine.

Anxiety belied her shaky confidence as she walked into the cool, pleasant interior of the shop. "Doogie?" she said.

"In your office," Pat, the assistant manager, told her.

Stephanie hurried toward the back. No surge of satisfaction filled her as it usually did when she walked through her little kingdom, as Clay had once called it.

Passing the curtained dressing rooms, she entered the back hallway and went into the office, which was piled high with catalogs and samples. Her son sat in a wing chair, one leg thrown over the arm in a careless position. She noticed his sneakers were wearing thin. He'd soon have a hole under the ball of his big toe. She sighed. Twelve-year-olds went through everything—clothes, shoes and food—so fast.

"I just spoke to Officer Dorelli," she said, slipping into her chair behind the desk. She hooked a strand of hair behind her ear and looked at her son. Really looked at him.

He was more than cute. He already showed the lanky form of her family and the stunning good looks of his father. His hair was dark, almost black, and he had brilliant blue eyes, a true blue, unlike hers that had a dusky gray tint.

Doogie swallowed, but he said nothing.

"Well?" she demanded, suppressing an urge to bawl like a baby rather than act the reasonable parent.

She didn't want to deal with this on top of worrying about money, mortgage payments and keeping the store profits up in face of each downward turn in the economy. She didn't need the constant reminder of her youth and its romantic, idealistic dreams, as personified by Nick Dorelli, invading her peace of mind. Life could be cruel....

"What have you got to say for yourself?" she asked her son.

"Nothing."

"Nothing? You're caught shoplifting and you have nothing to say?" The silence stretched between them. "Why?"

He shrugged. "I wasn't gonna keep it. It was...well, like I just wanted to watch it, then I'd have brought it back."

"You could have rented it. You got your allowance this morning. Why didn't you do that?"

He squinched his face up as if thinking about it was really hard. She noticed the smoothness of his skin, how tan he was already this year, except for a scar running from the edge of his chin down under the line of jawbone. He'd fallen and split his chin open on a skateboard last year.

When he'd walked in the door of the shop, blood running down the front of his T-shirt like a river, her heart had stopped. She'd taken him to the emergency clinic where they'd put eight stitches in to close the cut. Had anyone ever remarked on the difficulties of raising a child alone?

The sardonic humor helped keep the despair at bay. She had a million things to do to get the store ready for the Summer Madness sale coming up next week. Time was a pit bull, always snapping at her heels.

"Doogie?"

"There was a line. It was too much hassle." He shrugged, defiant as only an adolescent can be.

"Hassle," she repeated. She tried to be calm, to speak without accusation in her voice. They had to get to the bottom of this. "Shoplifting isn't a minor infraction or a fight with a friend. It's stealing."

"I wasn't stealing. I'd have brought it back tomorrow."

"Taking something without permission is wrong, no matter what your intentions might be." Nausea gripped her as she tried to speak reasonably and appeal to his finer qualities. "Think how you would feel if Clyde took your baseball mitt without asking you first. You'd think some-one had stolen it."

"Clyde's a dork."

She remembered the two boys were no longer friends. "But think how you'd feel," she persisted. She had to get through to him somehow. "You'd be hurt. And angry. That's how I feel."

He kept his gaze fixed on the floor at his feet, looking very much like his father when she'd tried to talk to him about the problems in their marriage. Men. They never wanted to hear the bad stuff, only the good.

"Think about how you would have felt if it had been your father who had answered the call and found his son was accused of shoplifting. Think about how he would have felt."

Two circles of shame formed in the boy's cheeks. Good. Maybe her words were getting through to him. His father had been one of the best deputies in the county. He'd died a hero, leaping in front of a bullet which would have hit a woman holding a child. His bullet-proof vest deflected the first shot, but not the second that went in his neck. He'd bled to death before the paramedics arrived.

Doogie didn't stir from his sullen position. She felt an

upsurge of fear and helplessness. "Well?" she demanded. "What have you got to say for yourself?"

He stared at the floor.

"You will return to Mrs. Withers tomorrow," she decided.

He blinked at that. "I don't need a baby-sitter."

"A person who can't be trusted out on his own does." She caught sight of her face in the decorative mirror on a highboy beside the door. She saw desperation in her eyes and willed it away with an effort. "This was a trial period, remember? You said you wouldn't be bored here at the office."

"I'm not bored." His mouth pulled down at the corners while his bottom lip puckered stubbornly.

She took a breath and spoke firmly. "What happened this morning tells me I was wrong to listen to your arguments."

"It was just a dumb video. It didn't mean anything. I'll never do it again." His voice, deeper of late, segued into a treble. He gestured with his hand, a quick, angry flick as if to throw out her statement.

His hands were large, more those of a man than a child. He was growing up. Twelve years old and he was only three inches shorter than she was. In another couple of years, he'd be as tall...and much stronger.

If she couldn't use words and reasoning to control him now, what would she do then?

"You'll go back to Mrs. Withers for the rest of the month. And you're grounded for that time."

His mouth opened in protest.

She continued. "You'll also apologize to the store owner—"

"I already did. Nick...Deputy Dorelli...made me before he brought me over here."

Stephanie frowned at this news. She wished Nick hadn't been the one to answer the call on her son. It was embarrassing. However, she could handle it and anything else that came up. Being married to a policeman, she'd had to.

Her husband had loved his job. He'd loved the uniform and the camaraderie with his deputy buddies. He'd worked a lot of overtime so they could save up enough money for repairs, then he'd used every spare minute to fix up the small ranch she'd inherited. Those early years had been the best part of their marriage. She tried not to think of the later years.

"Can I go now?"

"No. You'll stay here until the store closes at six. You should have brought something to read." She hesitated. "Trust is a funny thing. It's given automatically to those we love, but when it's breached, you have to earn it. Your father would have been very disappointed—"

"I don't care," he muttered. He stood, shoving the chair back with his legs. "I don't care what he would have thought. He wasn't…he wasn't…I don't care."

The *pop* of her hand against his cheek reverberated through the silent office for long seconds after the act.

Stephanie, leaning across her desk, stared as the red imprint formed on her son's face. Tears welled in his shocked, disbelieving eyes. He'd never been struck in his life, other than his fight with Clyde. She couldn't believe it herself. She'd never hit another person.

Doogie leapt to his feet and turned from her, his hands balled into fists. He made a loop of his arms against the wall and hid his face inside it. For all his lanky height, he looked like what he was—a kid who was in trouble, young and vulnerable, scared, defiant and sorry, all at the same time.

Stephanie straightened slowly, feeling as old and wicked as the witch from *Snow White*. She sank into her chair as the tremors started, earthquakes of emotion that she couldn't control. "Doogie, I'm sorry. It was wrong of me to strike you."

He made a muffled sound, then turned and ran, crashing through the outside door and cutting across the parking lot in front of an elderly couple, nearly knocking them down as he fled the place.

Stephanie stood, her mind in a whirl. She clenched a hand over her stomach and felt totally helpless in dealing with her son. She was aware of the disapproving glances from the couple as she stared outside. She nodded apologetically to them and closed the door.

For a moment she thought she was going to be sick. The tinkle of chimes at the front door reminded her she had a full afternoon of work ahead and Pat hadn't had lunch yet.

Worried, her heart aching, she went to the front. "Ready for a lunch break?" she asked with forced cheer.

"Starved," Pat affirmed. "Everything okay with the kid?" She'd known Doogie since birth, had, in fact, babysat with him when she'd still been a girl in school.

"No. Did he say anything to you?"

Pat shook her head, her smile sympathetic. "I saw Nick Dorelli drop him off at the door. I knew he must be in trouble." She hesitated. "Don't be too hard on him. All kids go through a stage, well, you know..." She grabbed her purse, tilted her head in the direction of two teenage girls going over the racks of earrings on a carousel, and left.

Stephanie straightened a shelf of cotton sweaters, then surveyed the small shop. The Glass Slipper looked smart, up-to-the-minute and friendly. She'd picked the muted gray-green of sage and the soft yellows and red of the local clay for a theme. Pedestals of black Colorado granite held inexpensive urns that looked priceless. Scarves and costume jewelry were casually draped over the clay pieces.

The ordered disarray didn't comfort her today. She sighed and rubbed her forehead where a headache was making itself known. Anger and embarrassment with her son roiled in her. She felt incompetent as a parent. Maybe she was.

Giggles from the two girls brought her back to the business at hand. She dredged up a smile. "Those look lovely on you," she said to one who'd put on a pair of earrings from the rack. "Do you want them wrapped or are you going to wear them?"

"I'll wear them." The girls paid and left, talking and giggling about a boy one of them liked.

Once she'd been that carefree, but not since the summer she'd graduated and her mother had divorced her father and moved to Santa Fe, leaving them behind, Stephanie reflected.

She'd started her first year at the community college while Nick went east to a big university. In January her father had gone hunting and died in an avalanche.

Clay Bolt had been the deputy who'd come to tell her. He'd been with her when they dug her father out. He'd gone to the morgue with her. He'd stayed at the house until her mother arrived. After the funeral, Stephanie had lived there alone.

Nick had come home at spring vacation and seen Clay with her on the porch, the deputy's arms around her to comfort her at a low moment in her life. Nick had accused her of betraying him.

She'd been astounded, then furious that he didn't trust

her, when she'd trusted him at his Ivy League school with all those debutantes hanging around. After he'd stormed out, she'd waited for him to come back to apologize, but he hadn't. Not one call, one letter. She'd stubbornly resisted the need to contact him.

Until Clay's death, she'd thought nothing could have been worse than that bleak period. The following year had been the loneliest of her life. Clay had become her closest friend. Months later, accepting that it was over between her and Nick, she'd dated the handsome deputy. They'd married a year after that.

Her husband had been even-tempered, a man who liked working with his hands, either on the house or on the various vehicles they'd had. The marriage had had its off moments, but mostly it had been good.

She sighed shakily. Always, always, she would regret that stupid quarrel before he'd gone off to work. He'd stopped at the convenience store to pick up a pack of gum because he'd quit smoking and had run into a robbery in progress.

Sometimes she felt as if her life had ended that day, too. But she'd had a child to care for, and that alone was enough to make her go on.

The death had changed Doogie, though. He'd become quieter and harder to handle; difficult where once he'd been easygoing and good-humored; moody where once he'd been mischievous and given to joking.

If only she had a man who could talk to Doogie like a father. Doogie had adored Clay. The two males had been close.

She stewed over the situation the rest of the afternoon. When the store closed at five and Doogie hadn't returned, she paced the tiny office, unsure what to do.

The mayor's wife, who was also her partner in the store, breezed in. "Hi. How's it going?"

"Hi, Amy. Fine. It was slow this afternoon."

"Everyone's waiting for the Summer Madness sales to start. Did all our merchandise come in?"

"Not yet, but I'm expecting it Monday."

She and Amy had opened the store four years ago. And she and Clay had quarreled about it ever since. He had liked his wife at home, not in town until all hours, as he put it. Actually the store was open late only on Friday night.

"Good." Amy picked up a package under the counter. "Pat said my new outfit was in. You should get yourself one of these silk gown and peignoir sets," she advised. "You never know when you might want to seduce a man. That's what I'm going to do to the mayor tonight." Laughing, she took her package and said good-night.

Stephanie's smile dried up as soon as the door closed. She hadn't thought of seducing a man in a long time. That was way down on her list of priorities. Right now, she was a parent with a missing child. After another half hour, she gave up her troubled vigil and picked up the phone. She called the dispatcher and asked for Deputy Dorelli.

Chapter Two

Ten minutes later, Stephanie stood at the barred window and watched as Nick stepped down from the cruiser and crossed the parking lot. He walked with the easy assurance of a man who knew his world and was secure in it.

Gone was the young man she'd once known. He hadn't been that person in years, but it wasn't until last Christmas, under a sprig of mistletoe, that she'd fully realized it.

That kiss had shaken her. It had stirred passion and longing and memories of the past that she hadn't allowed herself to consider in years. With it had come the startling realization that she was still a woman and she still had a heart full of dreams. She blinked as unexpected tears stung her eyes.

Nick entered without knocking and got right to the point. "What's wrong?"

For the wildest second, she thought of being enfolded in his comforting embrace. She forced her mind back to the real world. "It's Doogie. He and I...we quarreled...about the video." She couldn't bring herself to call the problem by its name. "He ran off—"

"What time was that?"

"Noon. I haven't seen him since. I thought he would come back to the shop when he calmed down." She pressed her lips together as worry ate at her.

Nick shrugged, his expression calm. "He's probably too ashamed to face you."

She blurted out the rest of it. "I slapped him. I never have before. I...it just happened. Oh, Nick, if you'd seen his face. He was so upset."

"Easy, Steph," he said in a quiet tone.

Once she'd loved his voice with its deep cadence that could be soothing or exciting, according to the circumstances. Once just the sound of it over the phone had made her heart pound.

His gaze caught and held hers. Instead of their opaque darkness, she sensed emotions in him that she hadn't been aware of in a long time. She also saw the wariness.

"Did you call the ranch and see if he maybe hitched a ride home? That would be my bet on where he is," he said with a businesslike brevity.

"I've called every half hour. This isn't like him. He's always been—" A sob caught in her throat.

"Easy," he said again in his patient-cop mode. "Stay put. I'll cruise around and see if I can find him."

"I can help. I'll look...." She tried to think where a twelve-year-old would go. "He wouldn't go to Clyde's, would he?" She looked at Nick for his opinion.

"He might. Have you tried there?"

She shook her head, already reaching for the phone. The call revealed that Clyde was spending the night with a friend and his mother hadn't seen Doogie in a week.

"Not there," she said in a croak, hanging up. The sky

seemed darker when she gazed out the window, hoping
to see the lanky figure of her son coming back. "The sun
is setting."

A hand closed on her shoulder. She resisted the urge
to lay her cheek against it and soak up the warmth. He'd
been like this after her father's death—kind, considerate,
concerned about her well-being.

"It won't be dark for hours yet. Walk over to the
school. He might be hanging around there. I'll check with
you in, say, half an hour?"

"All right." After he left, she grabbed her purse and
locked up. She walked as fast as she could to the school.
There wasn't a soul around. Even the janitor had gone for
the day.

Tears balled in her throat. If he was hurt...if something
happened... It would be her fault. She should have remained calm. That was a mother's job, to be calm and
guide her child on the right path.

She rushed along the nearly deserted Main Street, her
thoughts going in every direction. One of them shocked
her. If she and Nick had married, if Doogie was their son,
she wondered how things might have been different.

Dear heavens...

Nick's cruiser was in the parking lot when she arrived.
She pressed a hand to her heart. Doogie was with him.

Too overcome to speak, she nodded, unlocked the office door and went inside. Doogie followed. He looked
scared and defiant, but his eyes were worried and his
mouth was pinched in at the corners.

Unexpected tears rolled down her face. She folded her
arms on the cluttered desk surface and wept in silent misery.

After a minute, arms glided around her middle. She

raised up and clasped Doogie to her breast. His tears fell with hers.

"I'm sorry, Mom. I'm sorry. Please, please don't..."

She cupped his face in her hands. "You must promise me never, never to do anything like that again. Promise."

"I won't. Never. Honest."

She hugged him to her, fear eating holes in her stomach. She must be raising him wrong for this to happen, but she didn't know how she could do better. She needed advice, someone who understood boys and could talk to Doogie.

A picture of Nick, his keen gaze peering all the way to her soul, came to her. Her breath caught in her throat. Not him.

At Christmas, he'd been cynical and hard when he'd taunted her about being the grieving widow. This after he'd kissed her nearly mindless. She'd been furious...and excited and totally confused.

Her son stirred in her arms. She released him and grabbed a tissue for each of them. He wiped his eyes and blew his nose, then moved away from her.

She didn't try to hold him. There was something older and infinitely sadder in the depths of her son's eyes, as if a part of his childhood had been ripped away from him in the hours he'd been gone. It hurt her.

"Where did you go?"

"Nowhere, just walked around." His voice cracked. "Then I tried to thumb a ride home."

Just as Nick had thought he would.

"I have to thank Deputy Dorelli," she said, recalling they'd left him in the parking lot.

When she went out, the cruiser was gone. He'd brought her son back, then thoughtfully left them alone. She stood in the last warm rays of sunlight, not sure what she felt.

Since Christmas, something had changed between her and Nick. He made her uneasy with his unrelenting gaze, as if he'd weighed her worth and she came up a full pound short.

She drew a shaky breath and turned to her son. "Let's go home, shall we?"

"Yeah, we've got to check the stock."

"Right. 'On a ranch, the chores are never done—'"

"'Just caught up for the moment,'" Doogie finished the often-quoted lecture from his father.

Later, thinking over the long day, Stephanie decided she'd overreacted. She inhaled the sage-scented air. Her son was in bed, she had a successful business, all was right with her world.

So why did she feel so miserable?

Stephanie dropped the day's receipts into the after-hours depository at the bank with a weary sigh. The Summer Madness sale was over, thank heavens. For six days, from Monday until one o'clock today, they'd been swamped by customers. She and Pat and Amy had put in long hours this week.

Not that she was complaining. They'd moved a lot of merchandise. The new line of jewelry they'd decided to try had done very well. She'd already ordered more of it.

Stopping by her car, she viewed the Saturday traffic, which was light. She had to go to the grocery, but first she'd have lunch before going home to her recalcitrant son.

The week had been a terrible one. They'd hardly spoken to each other. He'd resented going to the sitter's house, and she had missed having him at the shop. They could certainly have used his help. However, she had to stick to her guns.

To have rescinded his punishment would have meant she could be maneuvered into changing her mind or that she didn't think shoplifting a serious offense. He might have gotten the idea he could do as he darned well pleased.

But it had been a hard week. He didn't speak unless spoken to, and then, as briefly as possible. She'd left him at the ranch doing chores that morning.

A truck, one of those sports utility vehicles that the sheriff's department used, turned the corner. She recognized the dark hair and wide shoulders even from a distance. She quickly climbed into her car and drove off.

She didn't want Nick to see her standing on the sidewalk, unable to make up her mind about what to do on a Saturday afternoon and dreading the weekend. He would probably go to the Bear Tooth Saloon that evening. It was the local hangout for singles. She drove down the block, trying to decide what she wanted to eat.

She quietly sighed. She really was beat. She'd get her groceries and head home. She pulled into the parking lot at the only shopping mall located in the town and stopped. Her gaze fell on the new deli that had recently opened.

A sign in the window proclaimed the special of the day was a soup and salad combo. That sounded good.

The air-conditioning hit her with a pleasantly chilling blast when she went inside. It was unusually hot for June. She called a greeting to the waitress, who'd been two years behind her in school. "Hi, Peg. How's it going?"

"Hi. We're busy today. You alone?"

"Yes."

The first person she spotted when Peg led her to a table was her nemesis. Nick was seated at a booth with an adorable blonde who leaned against his shoulder and gave him a kiss on the cheek while Stephanie watched, her eyes going wide.

He smiled and playfully tugged at a golden curl that brushed his chin. When he looked up, his eyes met hers.

She didn't look away fast enough. He nodded a greeting, then glanced around at the restaurant. The place was full and a line was forming for tables. He gestured to the banquette opposite him and his dinner partner.

The waitress, who knew both of them, noticed the invitation. "Do you want to sit with Nick?" she asked. "That way you won't be alone, and it'll free up a table for someone else."

Stephanie remembered a time when she'd been alone and had longed for his company. She'd faithfully waited for him, for all the good that had done her. Ah, well, she could stand his company for one meal, she decided grimly. "Okay."

She followed the younger woman across the room and slipped into the seat opposite Nick and the cute blonde. "I don't think I've met your date," she said, her smile real this time.

"Nikki, meet Stephanie. Stephanie, this is my favorite niece, Nikki Carradine."

The four-year-old dimpled into a charming smile. "I think you're pretty," she said to Stephanie. "I've got a boyfriend," she confided. "His name is Zach. Do you have one?"

Stephanie felt a blush warm her ears. "Not at the present."

"Uncle Nick doesn't have a girlfriend," she continued. "I was going to marry him, but Momma said I have to marry somebody my age. How old are you?"

"Nikki, it isn't polite to ask a lady her age," Nick

chided with a gentle smile that did things to Stephanie's heart.

"Why not?"

His brows drew together. "I'm not sure, but I think Nonna said it wasn't done, and I always believed her."

"I'm the same age as your uncle," Stephanie told the pretty youngster, ignoring her escort.

"Do you have a little girl?"

"No. I have a twelve-year-old son."

"Is he nice?"

"Most of the time."

Nikki looked at her uncle with a question in her beautiful blue eyes. Stephanie remembered that her father, an attorney in Denver, had blond hair and blue eyes.

"A little old for you. Better stick with Zach. He's in her Sunday School class," Nick explained to Steph.

"But I'm not going to marry him," Nikki declared.

Talk of marriage made Stephanie uncomfortable. She tried to avoid looking at Nick, all but impossible since he sat directly across the table from her. She was acutely aware of his dark chocolate eyes flashing from one person to another as he followed the conversation. He wore a slightly skewed, definitely sardonic, grin.

The waitress came for their order. When she left, there was an awkward lull in the conversation.

"How was the Summer Madness sale?" Nick asked.

"Fine. Busy." She took a sip of water.

His foot brushed hers under the table. "Sorry."

Tingles floated up her leg. "That's okay."

"Uncle Nick, I need to go potty," Nikki announced.

"Sure thing, sport." He stood and held out his hand to help his niece jump down from the banquette.

He wore a neatly pressed, long-sleeved white shirt, the cuffs rolled up a couple of turns, jeans with a sharp crease and dress boots. Since he lived in bachelor quarters in town, and she felt certain he didn't iron his own things, she assumed he sent his clothes to the laundry.

"Would you like me to take her?" Stephanie asked.

"Would you mind? I always stand outside the door, feeling like some kind of weirdo while I wait." He grinned in that lopsided manner that had once seared right into her heart.

Nikki placed her hand trustfully in Stephanie's. She chattered about her favorite things to eat while they wound their way to the back of the restaurant.

When Stephanie spoke to people she knew, they smiled at her and invariably glanced toward the booth where Nick sat. Heat seeped into her cheeks. In a small town, memories were long. The townsfolk would recall that she and Nick had once been inseparable. She'd thought they would one day be a family....

When she and Nikki returned to the table, she found Nick talking to a friend in the next booth about the soccer season and how it was going. He finished and stood to let his niece back into her seat.

"We can use another player on the team," he mentioned. "Doogie might be interested. We practice three afternoons a week and play on Saturday afternoon over at the high school."

"He can't. Doogie is on restriction the rest of the month." She spoke calmly in the face of Nick's frowning perusal. "That's another ten days."

"Maybe later," Nick put in easily.

"Is Doogie being punished?" Nikki wanted to know.

"Yes. He did something he wasn't supposed to, and now he's grounded." She avoided Nick's eyes.

Their order arrived, the house specialty burgers for

Nick and his niece, a salad with a grilled chicken sandwich for her.

"Hmm, maybe we'd better put something over that pretty dress," Nick mused. "We wouldn't want to get mustard on it. How about my handkerchief?"

"Okay," Nikki said agreeably. She let him tuck a white hankie under her chin. "This was my Easter dress."

"It's very nice," Stephanie said.

"Mom and I saw the Easter Bunny at the store." She clapped a hand over her mouth and giggled. "You know something? It wasn't him. It was a man pretending to be the Easter Bunny." With an indignant huff, she confided, "He had glasses. Everybody knows rabbits don't need glasses. They eat lots of carrots."

Nick and Stephanie laughed at the end of this charming tale, told with great earnestness and a precise knowledge of the Easter Bunny and his ways.

Stephanie's laughter died when she found Nick's narrowed gaze on her. Hungry eyes. Her breath strangled in her throat. She couldn't breathe or think or tear her gaze away.

"Pass the ketchup, please," Nikki said, breaking into the turbulent moment.

Nick glanced away from her and passed the bottle over. When he looked at Stephanie again, she went hazy with relief. She'd been mistaken in what he was thinking. He was utterly calm, as cool as shaved ice, the way he normally was...except for that one incident in Amy's kitchen.

"It's going to be a hot summer, it seems," she said. "The news said the high temperatures last week set a new record." A blush crawled up her neck. Brilliant conversation.

"Yeah, I heard the same on TV this morning. I hope it isn't true. We don't need that problem this summer."

"Are you expecting others?"

"The highway will be resurfaced down to Denver next month. It'll slow traffic. The tourists will get grouchy. There'll be some fender benders because of it and probably some fist fights." He gave a snort of laughter. "Business as usual."

"Do we still have more crime in the summer than in the winter?" she asked. She missed knowing the details of life around her, she realized. Being a cop's wife, she used to know everything that happened in the county.

"Yes, mostly vandalism. Some petty stealing. In cow country, you get rustling, but we haven't had anything major in a couple of years. No murders or grand larceny."

"Have there been any bank robberies?" Nikki asked.

"Not lately," he said with a grin at her avid interest. "The last big thing was the break-in at the summer house where that diamond necklace was taken. That was a couple of years ago." Nick saw Steph's eyes darken and could have kicked himself. Clay had been killed during a robbery at a quick market right after that. "The county is pretty quiet."

She ducked her head over her plate and ate busily. Nick sighed internally. He knew Steph had been horrified and embarrassed at her son's brush with the law. There was no need to embarrass her further with talk of crime.

He cut Nikki's hamburger into quarters, saw that she had ketchup for her fries, then added some to his own plate. Across from him, Stephanie ate without enthusiasm. If it had been left to her, he thought, she'd have chosen not to sit with him.

They'd managed to avoid each other for most of the years since he'd returned from college, as much as one could in a place that size. Until last Christmas, they'd managed to be polite, cordial even.

When they'd split up, he remembered, she'd acted as if she'd been the hurt party and he the guilty culprit. She'd never forgiven him for distrusting her, but with the rumors of her infidelity confirmed, what did she expect? He'd waited for her to explain, to make him see how she could let another man hold her, but she hadn't.

The memory rekindled his anger. He tamped it down. Their time together had been a lifetime ago.

A kid two tables over banged a spoon on the high chair tray. He wanted to go over and arrest the parents for letting him disturb the peace. "Did you sell out of everything in the store this week?" he asked.

"Nearly."

"Amy said it was one of the best weeks you'd ever had."

"It was. I was nervous about some new jewelry we'd ordered, but it went over very well."

"Those earrings you're wearing are real pretty. Were they part of the new stuff?"

The earrings looked like tiny sunbursts hanging from her ears. When she reached up and touched one, he remembered what it had been like to be able to kiss her right below the filigree of gold. He shut that thought off pronto.

"Yes. We ordered from a company in Reno. Their designer, a Native American named Jackson Firebird, did them. He's getting quite a reputation."

Nick couldn't keep his eyes off her mouth and the tiny mole near it. Each word hit him like a caress, reminding him of things he'd forced himself to forget. When she talked about her ideas for expanding the shop, she actually became animated, something that hadn't happened in his presence for years.

Stephanie, he realized, was very much like his sister, Dina, a CPA with her own business in Denver. Dina had just had a new daughter, which was why he'd gone down and picked up Nikki for the weekend. He'd figured Nikki needed some extra attention and Dina needed all the rest she could get. Besides, he liked kids, had always figured on having a passel of 'em.

With this woman.

He set his jaw and focused on the conversation. The anger faded somewhat as he listened. Steph had sound business sense. A modern woman with a mind of her own.

Clay, he suddenly remembered, hadn't liked his wife working. He'd resented the success of the shop. Nick had counseled him to accept and encourage Stephanie's interest in the store, knowing from talking to Dina that women sometimes needed more than a husband and a family to keep them occupied.

"If you need an accountant or an attorney," he told her, "I've got an 'in' with some good ones."

"Amy and I were talking about that this morning and decided to let someone else do the taxes in the future. It's too much for us. We've decided to use the new guy in town, but thanks, anyway," she said politely, making it clear she needed no helpful suggestions from him.

"I ate half my dinner, Uncle Nick. Is that enough?"

"Uh, yeah, that's fine."

"What do we get for dessert?"

"The sky's the limit, kiddo. Name it."

"We could share a banana split," she said hopefully.

"You got it." He glanced across the table. "How about you? Can you hold a banana split?"

"Well..."

Nick willed her to agree. Stephanie was too serious. She needed to relax and enjoy some of the simple pleasures of life.

Whoa, boy, back off, he warned himself.

"That sounds wonderful. Fattening, but wonderful," she finally acquiesced with a little trill of laughter.

It went right to his head. And other places.

When their treat was served, they dug in. He let Nikki eat her fill, then he finished it off. Stephanie ate half of hers. He finished it off, too. Nick was aware of her eyes on him.

"What?" he demanded. "Do I have ice cream on my chin or something?"

"I was wondering if you ever got filled up."

"Nope. I have a hollow leg, right, Nikki?"

"Momma said I have one, too," Nikki piped up. "She said I was just like you, Uncle Nick."

Stephanie's laughter pealed out again. He grinned ruefully. "Well, there are worse things you could be," he said with great self-righteousness.

Nick cruised the two-lane section of the highway until the traffic flow was a smooth sixty-five. As soon as he exited, he knew it would speed back up except for a few pokies who would bunch up and irritate drivers who were trapped behind them and wanted to zip ahead. He took the last Off ramp into town.

His regular duties didn't include highway patrol, but he filled in for vacationing deputies during the summer. He headed for the station. His shift was over, but he wanted to check out a misdemeanor reported earlier.

No one was in except the dispatcher. "The sheriff's gone to talk to the mayor. He won't be back unless it's an emergency,'' the old man, a semiretired deputy, told him.

"Who was on the misdemeanor reported this afternoon?''

"Thurman.''

"Who'd he pick up?''

"Nobody. Two boys were trying to grab some tires outside a garage. They scattered when Thurman showed up.''

"They were on foot?''

"Yeah. Thurman figured they needed a set of tires to get back in action. Said they looked about sixteen or seventeen.''

Nick didn't acknowledge the sense of relief that made him feel ten pounds lighter. Steph would have grounded her son for life if he'd been involved. "I'm heading out. See you in the morning.''

The old deputy waved to him while he answered a call. Nick lingered to see if he would be needed. The dispatcher shook his head to tell him it wasn't an emergency.

In the cruiser once more, Nick drove slowly along the main street of the town. Most of the shops were closed. Thursday evening wasn't a big night on the town for the local folks.

There was one shop whose window displayed a Closed sign, but a light burned in the back. Stephanie's compact sedan was in the parking lot next door. She was working late. He drove past and turned down a side street.

At a turn-of-the-century Victorian, Nick saw Doogie sitting on the steps, his chin in his hands, his elbows on his knees, waiting for his mom. Two much younger children chased each other in the yard. Mrs. Withers sat on the porch swing and watched them.

A car stopped at the curb. The two kids rushed to greet

their father, who scooped them both up into a hug. He
talked to the baby-sitter for a minute before leaving to
pick up his wife at the county courthouse where she
worked.

Nick headed back for Main Street and the heart of
town, hoping to catch Stephanie before she left the office.
He had a thing or two to say to her and, by damn, he was
going to say them.

Chapter Three

Steph's car was still parked in the lot next door when Nick arrived. He wheeled in beside it and headed for the back of the store. With his fist balled, he banged on the door.

"Who is it?" Stephanie's voice called out a second later.

"Nick."

He resented the cautious way she opened the door, as if she expected a trick or maybe an attack.

"Yes? Is something wrong?" She glanced out at her car.

"Not as long as you cooperate. We need to talk."

She appeared confused. "Well, I suppose I can. I just finished the books. What do you want to talk about?"

He took hold of the door and pushed his way inside. She didn't resist, but her eyes changed from questioning to wary in a blink. She should be wary. He was damned irritated.

"About Doogie," he added, going into her office and sitting in a wing chair across from her desk.

She followed more slowly and took her seat. "What about him?" It was clear she didn't want advice.

"I want him on the team."

Hooking her hair behind her ear, she stared at him as if unable to comprehend his words.

"The soccer team," he clarified. "I want him to join the soccer team that I coach."

"Why?"

"Because he needs it."

"Really?" Her tone chilled. She picked up a pencil and tapped the eraser end on the desk.

"Yes, really." He took a breath and suppressed the sarcastic remarks he wanted to utter. "He's not a six-year-old. He needs to be with kids his own age. He needs action...and rules, the safety of the sport to work out his aggressions—"

She flung down the pencil and stood. With her knuckles hitched on her hips, she demanded, "Who are you to tell me what my son needs?"

He stood and straightened to his full six-one height, which didn't intimidate her one whit. "I'm a man. I've gone through puberty and all the frustrations and upheavals that brings."

"But you've never been married or had children. You've never had to raise a child on your own."

"No," he agreed. "I haven't."

The office was tiny and held her scent—a sweet, breezy perfume with a hint of sultry passion and tangy bite in it. He wanted to gather her into his arms and rediscover all the secret places she touched it to her skin.

"Well, as they say, until you've tried it, don't knock it, or in this case, don't tell others how to do it." She pulled her mouth in at the corners when she was angry, causing her lips to sort of bunch together. It reminded him of Nikki puckering up for a kiss. Only the kiss wouldn't be anything like his niece's if Stephanie did it. Heat broke loose in him.

He hooked his thumbs in his belt. "I took a master's degree in psychology along with law enforcement. I've worked with youths for ten years. I've seen how they get in trouble. Doogie is headed for trouble."

"That's why he's at Mrs. Withers's."

"That's why he's going to get in deeper."

She glared at him. He held the look.

At last she unfolded her hands and let them slide from her hips. When she sank into the chair, he sat in the wing chair again, his forearms resting across his knees as he leaned forward. "Let me work with him for a while. He needs boys his own age to wrestle with and maybe talk to. He might tell me what's bothering him."

"How do you know something's bothering him?" She pushed a hand through her hair in an agitated manner.

Nick shrugged, but said nothing. He wondered why he was there. She'd made it plainer than a mean cow with a sore tail she didn't want him butting into her life. A man would be a fool to get involved with a woman who'd already cast him aside once. Her voice brought him back to the matter at hand.

"When we had the quarrel over the video, I reminded him of how terrible his father would have felt if he'd known. Doogie said he didn't care and stormed out. How could he not care? He adored his father. Clay adored him."

Nick stood and went to the small, barred window at the back wall, shutting out the pain and confusion in her beautiful eyes. He watched the sun rays dance on the drops of water misting up from the car wash behind the shopping center.

"It isn't enough." He turned to Stephanie. "Memories aren't enough to live on."

She lifted her chin. "No one said they were."

"You act like you're trying. It's been two years, Steph. You've got to loosen the apron strings on the boy."

She looked so affronted, he half expected her to slap him. Instead she asked, "How?" Her lips trembled.

He wanted to cover them with his own and make her forget that she'd ever preferred another man to him.

He jerked back, startled at the thought.

"He can stay with the baby-sitter in the mornings," he suggested. "I'll pick him up at three on Monday, Wednesday and Thursday for practice. Our game is on Saturday. He can do some work at my place on the weekend. I'll pay him—"

"He can work here at the shop." She eyed him suspiciously. "What kind of work do you have for a boy?"

"Riding fences. Checking on the llamas I'm boarding for some dude from the city." He grinned. "Interesting critters, those llamas. Did you know they can spit just like a camel?"

She looked rather dazed at the change of subject.

"Well, how about the team? Make up your mind. I'm hungry. You want to go out to dinner?"

She shook her head. "I've got to pick Doogie up and go to the grocery. We have chores at home, the horses, the calves." She waved her hand vaguely.

"Are you going to let him on the team?" He carefully kept any trace of impatience from his voice.

"I...yes, I suppose it'll be all right. If he wants to."

"He does." He tipped a finger to his forehead and

headed for the door. No use pushing his luck with her. He'd got what he'd come for. He knew when to leave.

Stephanie sat in the chair, gently rocking back and forth for a few minutes after Nick left. Her mind was on her son and the estrangement between them for the past month. He seemed to resent everything she said to him, no matter how trivial.

Maybe Nick was right. Being around boys his own age might be the very thing he needed. She would see how it went. If his attitude didn't improve, it was back to Mrs. Withers with him.

After locking up, she drove the short distance to pick him up. He was sitting on the steps as usual. He sprang to his feet as soon as he saw her turn the corner and was ready to go when she stopped at the curb. Stephanie waved to Mrs. Withers and started off.

"I have some news," she commented.

"What is it?"

"I, um, talked to Officer Dorelli this afternoon. We have agreed that you can join the soccer team. If you're interested."

"I am," he said at once, as if afraid she'd change her mind if he didn't jump on it. "You said it was okay?"

Stephanie nodded. "Yes. I thought it sounded like fun."

"Yeah. He's the best coach in the county. His team wins the playoffs nearly every year. When do I start?"

"He's going to come by for you tomorrow. I'll call Mrs. Withers when we get home and tell her you'll stay with me." She paused. "I thought you could help out at the store for a couple of hours each day. You volunteered to do the vacuuming and dusting." She grinned. "The pay is minimal and you have to bank half your earnings."

"I will," he promised, a big grin on his face. Like his father's, his smile made her heart ache.

At the house he changed his clothes and went to the barn without a reminder. She heard him whistling as he fed calves and mucked out stalls. She felt something curiously like envy. She wished life was as simple as a soccer game.

Maybe it was. Maybe she'd lost.

Nick feinted right, then went left. Doogie stayed with him. When Nick let the ball drift in front of him, the kid was on top of it. He stole it and headed back down the field toward his goal.

"Good," Nick called. He glanced at his watch. Almost five. He'd been working with the boy for two hours. "You have sound moves. Good instincts, too."

Doogie nodded modestly, his attention trained on Nick as if he were delivering the wisdom of the ages. It made a man humble to be around kids.

"I played at school last year," Doogie explained.

"I'll keep you on the bench tomorrow afternoon, but you can suit up with us if you'd like."

"Sure."

Nick saw Doogie's ears go pink with pleasure. At the truck, he reached into the back, then tossed him a T-shirt with the team's name and logo—a growling bear—on it.

Doogie held it up. "Wow, neat."

"We usually wear black shorts, but anything will do. You got shin guards?"

"I'll get some."

"Okay. Let's get some supper. We can pick something up and eat at the store. I'll have your mom sign the necessary forms so you can play."

"Sure. Uh, what position do you think I ought to play once I start?"

"I like to move my players around so we get depth. That way any player can fill in for another if we need 'em. Families tend to go on vacations in the summer, you know?"

"Yeah."

Nick noticed the silence that ensued. Doogie was troubled about something. That was a fact.

He wondered what he would have done about the shoplifting episode if the boy had been his son. Would he have been as understanding as he was with another man's kid?

Absolute honesty forced him to admit he might not have been as keenly observant if Stephanie wasn't involved. He considered that idea for an unnerving moment. All right, he admitted it. He wanted her. He wondered if he was using the son as an excuse to see the mother.

Maybe he was, but there were other matters between them. The past, for one. The acute awareness for another. Maybe it was time to bury the hatchet and—and what?

With this in mind, he told Doogie they would pick up some supper and take it to Stephanie's boutique.

"That would be great."

He stopped at the Bear Tooth Saloon and bought pork barbecue sandwiches, curly french fries and, because Stephanie used to be a health freak, a big bowl of salad and one of fruit.

With a start, Nick realized he no longer knew her tastes, whereas once he'd known her as well as he'd known himself...or thought he had.

Doogie ran into the Main Street Market and picked up soft drinks, then Nick drove to the store on Main Street.

He waited at the back door while Doogie went through

the front of the store and into the office to let him in.
They spread out their feast. Doogie called his mom.

"Surprise. Dinner is served."

Stephanie closed the register and glanced at her son
with a questioning smile. He smiled back. His eyes
gleamed with pleasure. His sunny nature had returned.
She realized how much she had missed it.

"Dinner? Wow, I'm impressed," she said as they
walked to the back of the store. "I hope you remembered
the jelly. I'm starved."

His grin widened as she teased him about the dinner
he'd planned and executed all by himself when he'd been
four. She and Clay and Doogie had sat on the living room
rug and eaten the meal, which consisted of peanut butter
sandwiches, chocolate milk and two cookies each. Half-
way through, he had remembered he hadn't put any jelly
on the sandwiches. He'd taken the remains to the kitchen
and added the jelly before he let his parents finish. Remembering the jelly had become a family joke.

"Actually," he told her as they entered the hallway,
"Nick got everything."

"Nick?" Her steps slowed. "Is he in the office?"

"Yeah." Doogie's expression became anxious. "Is that
okay? I didn't think you'd mind."

What could she say? "Of course not. I was just surprised, that's all."

"He picked me up at Mrs. Withers today. We kicked
some balls around at the field. He gave me the team shirt.
I get to sit on the bench at the game tomorrow."

Stephanie digested all this news. She felt danger closing
in around her like a smothering fog. She couldn't figure
out the nervy way Nick made her feel.

Once he'd been the hero in her world, but that was long

ago. Now...now he was just a man, a cop like her husband had been. Nothing special in that.

Except that lately he made her nervous. Since that kiss under the mistletoe, she'd felt off balance around him, and she didn't like it. She kept remembering things she shouldn't. She thought he was, too. His eyes, when he looked at her...

She paused to collect herself before entering the office after her son. The desk was covered with napkins acting as place mats. Paper plates held curly fries and sandwiches still in their wrappers. Bowls of salad and fruit completed the meal. Nick sat in a straight chair at the corner of her desk. The wing chair was pulled up to the other end.

"How nice," she murmured. "Hello, Nick. Doogie tells me we have you to thank for dinner."

"It's pretty simple, but I thought it would be nice not to eat alone."

Did he think she was dying for his company? She sat at the desk chair and laid a napkin over her skirt. She added salad to her plate, using a plastic fork. "I thought all you eligible males went to the Bear Tooth on Friday nights to check out the action."

He shot her a quick perusal at the arch tone. "I go once in a while. I like to dance."

He'd danced with her at the Christmas party. And held her too close. She could still feel the heat from his powerful body washing over her in waves, making her dizzy and weak....

"Oh, yes, I remember," she said a shade too brightly. She picked up her fork and started to eat before she said something she'd regret. As usual, she felt defensive in his presence. He put her back up, as if they were continually battling over some undefined subject.

"Mom, uh, can we go shopping tonight? I have some money. I need a pair of soccer shoes."

"Lots of kids play in jogging shoes," Nick put in. He pushed a paper toward Stephanie. "You need to sign this."

Stephanie signed the parental permission form and remembered she hadn't bought Doogie new shoes yet. She'd noticed ages ago that he needed them. She removed a credit card from her purse and gave it to her son. "Get a new pair of sneakers, too. Those are practically gone."

"Great." Doogie wolfed down his meal.

She watched the two males as they ate. They talked about the upcoming soccer game and the team's prospects of winning the season. "Slim," Nick said, shaking his head. "Those Hogs are dynamite this year. They have mostly older guys. Next year, they'll have to rebuild from scratch when most of their team moves to the next league."

Doogie listened as if gold coated every word Nick spoke. Once he'd listened to his father that way. Now he seemed to resent it every time she mentioned Clay.

She sighed.

Dark eyes turned to her. Nick paused to study her for a second. It made her blood heat up, the way he could size up a person with that stare, which was sometimes hot, sometimes cool, but always disturbing.

"May I be excused?" Doogie asked, already rising.

She nodded. He grabbed up the credit card and took off. A moment of silence followed his departure. She was acutely aware that she and Nick were alone in the tiny office. She couldn't think of a thing to say.

"Doogie's a good player. He has a lot of natural ability," Nick commented. "I think he'll be a real asset to the team."

She nodded. They were alone in the store. She'd locked the front door and turned off the lights before coming to the office. Looking at the impromptu picnic, she was reminded of dates they'd shared all those years ago.

When she'd been young. And in love. With this man.

She wondered what they were doing here now and if it was wise to be with him. She recalled his strength when he'd lifted her into the truck, the scent of him—fresh as the outdoors, like pine forest and rich earth, a manly scent.

"Once we used to talk about everything under the sun," he mused aloud suddenly.

She glanced at him, then back at her food. It startled her that his thoughts apparently ran along the same lines as hers.

The past. It shaped the future whether one wanted it to or not. Guilt added to her inner turmoil. She had things to think about other than Nick. Her son, for one.

She recalled Doogie's animation as they ate. One afternoon with Nick, and her child glowed as if he'd been handed the moon.

Doogie was growing up. Nick had warned her of that, but he hadn't said how deserted she'd feel when her son also grew away from her. During the meal he'd taken his cues from Nick, wiping the orange-colored sauce that collected at the corners of his mouth after each bite, eating salad without her coaxing, all because Nick did.

Somehow this alarmed her. She'd kept everything as much the same as possible after Clay's death. Her own life had fallen apart after her father's death, and even before that, with her mother declaring she'd done her duty and now she was going to have her own life. Her mother worked in an art gallery in Santa Fe and loved it.

Stephanie sighed. She'd tried so hard to maintain a sense of equilibrium in their lives so that Doogie wouldn't feel his world had fallen apart the way hers had. Everyone needed a center. She'd tried to fulfill that role for Doogie.

"Dinner was very good," she said, laying her fork aside. "I should get back to work. I still have to close out the cash register. Thank you for helping Doogie today. It's kind of you to take an interest in him."

She nearly groaned aloud at how stilted she sounded.

"It was a pleasure. With his ability and some hard work, I think he can get a sports scholarship to college."

"You do?"

"Yeah," Nick answered. "I do. But he'd have to decide on a sport and stick with it."

"He likes soccer. Can a person get a scholarship in it?"

Nick shrugged. "I'm not sure. We can check. I think Doogie may grow tall enough for basketball, but he would have to bulk up a lot for football. Long and lean runs in your family."

"I don't want him playing football," Stephanie put in. "It's too rough."

"They wear all kinds of pads and things nowadays. It's safer than it used to be."

"You broke your collarbone—" She stopped speaking, but it was too late. She saw by the blaze in his eyes that he was recalling the incident at high school. She'd run onto the field when he'd gone down and had stayed with him while a local doctor had put a temporary splint on his arm. She'd gone to the hospital, too.

"People get hurt," she amended.

"Life doesn't come with guarantees," Nick told her, a hard undertone in the words. His dark eyes with their thick black lashes watched her relentlessly.

He made her feel as uncertain as a newborn, when he looked at her that way. He looked so tough and so sure he knew more of life than she did. He didn't.

Life had been relatively easy for him. He came from a nice family who'd been in the valley longer than dirt. He hadn't waited while the rescuers searched through tons of snow to find his father's frozen body. He hadn't spent countless lonely hours wishing time would pass so he could come to her. She had.

"But it does come with warnings," she said at last. She forced her attention to the present. "I've seen how rough sports can be. Doogie isn't going to play football."

Nick stood and stretched, then bundled their trash into the empty bag. "That's a ways down the road. Nothing has to be decided yet." He turned and did a hook over his head. The bag hit the bottom of the trash can without touching the sides.

She remembered his sinewy strength, the ropy agility of his body when he moved. He hadn't changed in that respect. But the young man she'd loved was gone. Now he seemed a powerful, threatening male, making her feel insecure in her efforts to guide her son on the straight and narrow.

"Thank you for the meal. What time is Doogie supposed to be at the school for the game tomorrow?"

"Around three. It'll start as soon after that as we can get everyone padded and ready. You should drop by and watch if you can spare the time. You might learn something."

She stiffened. There he went again, telling her she didn't know anything about raising a child. What had he been doing for the past twelve years while she was taking care of her son? Cruising around and having a good time, that's what. Other than one engagement three years ago, he'd played the field.

"Like what?"

He gave her another of those long, slow appraisals that

made her feel so uncertain. "That men like their women to watch when they're making like heroes."

The reply was so astounding she gaped at him before she could think of an answer. "Uhh. I have to go."

That was really brilliant. She thanked him again and said good-night, then rushed to the front of the store before she reminded him that once he'd been her hero...before he'd broken her heart with his distrust.

Stephanie held the bucket so the calf could reach the nipple easily. She absently scratched around the horn buds while the little one sucked noisily. The calf had been born two months later than the usual spring drop. It was a runt, as well.

"Nick says my speed is good. He wants me to work on control, especially in passing. Will you kick a few to me when we finish here?"

"Sure."

"We won yesterday. I wish I'd been on the field when you stopped by. You should have stayed for the ending. Nick says we might have a chance at the county championship. It would be a long shot but he says with me and Ty Murphy in the lineup, and if we don't lose anyone to an extended vacation or accident, then..."

Stephanie nodded as he talked on and on about Nick and the Bear Tooths. Weird name for a team, if anyone asked her. Which they didn't. At least, not her son. If it didn't come from the lips of that modern wonder, Nick Dorelli, it didn't count.

She finished with the calf, looked over their small herd, then leaned against the fence, her arms propped over the top rail. Her mare came over for an ear scratching and nuzzled her neck. Restlessness beat through her with the plangent urge of distant drums.

"After we kick a few balls, I thought I'd fix a sandwich, then head over to the river and fish until dark. Is that okay?" Doogie rinsed their buckets out at the spigot.

She nodded. Maybe she would go for a ride. The peace and quiet were getting to her. The house was a mile from town, set on its own sixty acres. Twenty cows and three horses grazed in the pasture. Not a car droned by this Sunday afternoon.

"I'll make sandwiches for both of us," she volunteered.

"Peanut butter?" he asked with a sly grin.

"Of course. With jelly."

They laughed. It sounded so wonderful, sharing laughter with her son. They kicked the soccer ball for thirty minutes, then went inside. The house held the warmth of the day. It felt good to her. A coldness had settled around her heart since Nick had shown up and informed her Doogie was a thief. A sigh escaped her. She'd wanted to crawl into bed and not come out.

However, she didn't live on memories as Nick had accused her of doing. Her husband was gone, and nothing could change that.

She squared her shoulders. She was alive. Very much so. She had the troubles to prove it. She grinned at her fatalistic humor. Things were better now. A month into soccer and Doogie was a different person. It smarted, but she had to admit she should thank Nick for the suggestion.

"Let's get with it," she ordered, heading to her room. "Last one to change has to eat liverwurst."

Doogie grabbed a loaf of bread. She got out the peanut butter. In his boots and jeans, with a baseball cap—worn backward, of course—he looked endearingly young and grown-up at the same time.

Her heart constricted with love. She pulled two packs

of chips from the pantry and added them along with two red delicious apples to their fare. He poured sodas for them.

Fifteen minutes later he was ready to be off, his fly rod and supplies in hand, a can of lemonade and a supply of fresh cookies in his tackle box. He didn't issue an invitation to her. Sensing that he wanted to be alone, she didn't mention going.

"I'll saddle up," he said in a voice that began as a tenor and ended as a baritone.

Puberty. Would they live through it?

She grinned at her own dramatic, albeit rhetorical, question. The late-afternoon sunshine was gentle, the breeze was playful, and all seemed well with the world.

Yeah, they'd make it through Doogie's teenage years. But nobody said it would be easy.

"I think I'll take a short ride," she decided. "Up to the lookout and back." She went to put on her riding boots.

When she returned, Doogie had her horse ready and was saddling Ringo, a contrary gelding that Clay had rescued from a dude ranch. Her mother's instinct urged her to tell her son he was not to ride the horse. Common sense overruled her heart. He knew horses and was an expert rider.

"He'll be restless" was all she let herself say.

"I can handle him," he replied in his new, gruff voice.

She nodded and mounted Cinderella. "Come on, Cindy-gal, let's get out of here." With a light touch of the reins, Stephanie set the mare on her way along the country road.

Behind her, she heard the pound of hooves as Doogie headed in the opposite direction. He let the gelding break into a run. Her mare could use some exercise, too. There was no traffic this far from town. She leaned forward. "Go, girl."

With a twitch of her ears, the mare stretched out, breaking into a running stride that was pure heaven. A rush of adrenaline took Stephanie by surprise. Giving in to it, she let the mare take the bit.

She laughed and hunkered down on Cindy's neck. The wind had blown the mane into a tangle. She rounded the curve and started up the long incline to the top of the hill where the lookout afforded a view of the valley and surrounding mountains. The mare tossed her head and pushed up the hill. They arrived at the scenic lookout, horse and rider puffing with exertion.

Pulling up, Stephanie came to a stop a couple of feet from the barrier railing. From the corner of her eye, Stephanie noted a movement. She swung around to the grove of pines that lined the side of the road and edged the clearing.

Her blood chilled when she saw what it was. *Mad dog.* The hair stood up on her scalp.

The animal was no more than ten feet away. It was actually a coyote. Foam stood on its lips. It swung its head toward her as it took two steps forward. Its hind legs wobbled under its weight, but it stayed upright.

In an eternity that was but a second, she realized the coyote was going to attack.

The mare, startled by the sight of the animal, backed into the railing. The coyote sprang. The mare reared and swung around. Stephanie sawed at the reins, trying to turn the animal and send her flying back down the road. The coyote came down under the mare's belly and snapped at the exposed underside.

Stephanie didn't stop to think. She kicked the mare,

causing her to lurch forward, bumping the coyote and
turning it aside. It came at them again.

The mare kicked out, catching a foot under the guard-
rail. She fell to her haunches. The coyote sprang to the
attack.

Stephanie, with deadly coldness, watched it as if in
slow motion. At the last second she kicked out with all
her might, catching the animal under the chin and sending
it crashing to the gravel.

The mare lunged upward, trying to stand in spite of its
injured leg. The action unseated Stephanie. She fell to the
ground with a *whuff* as the breath was knocked out of her.
Pain hit her in a giant wave. She ignored it.

She rolled away from thrashing hooves and the silent,
slobbering menace that watched them with red-rimmed
eyes. The mare squealed and wheeled to the side.

Stephanie tucked her left arm across her waist, barely
aware of pain in it. She grabbed a chunky rock in her
right hand and stood slowly. The coyote watched her
without moving.

Behind her, she was vaguely aware of the crunch of
gravel, of a motor running. Someone had stopped.

"Rabies," she called out. "Don't come close."

"Stand still," a masculine voice told her. It was as
calm as a placid sea, deep, soothing, utterly confident.
"Don't move a hair."

She froze in place, her eyes never leaving those of the
animal that stood, its head low, its ruff up, five feet away.
A shot rang out. The coyote jumped as if kicked by an
unseen foe. Its rear legs trembled and sank, then the front.
Blood dribbled from its mouth along with saliva. It died
without a whimper, its eyes open, looking at her.

She bent forward as darkness closed around her.

Chapter Four

Nick cursed and ran forward. "Get out of the way," he muttered when the mare acted skittish. He managed to grab the reins and lead the animal to the far end of the lookout. There he tied her in the shade and hurried back.

Giving the coyote a couple of prods with the gun barrel, Nick made sure the critter wasn't playing possum before turning his attention to Stephanie. He laid the rifle on the gravel and checked her pulse.

Too fast, but otherwise okay, he thought.

She moaned, one hand over her mouth, as she knelt on the gravel. He slipped an arm around her shoulders. "What were you going to do—fight the damned brute bare-handed?" he demanded.

The haze cleared from her eyes. "No. I was going to use this rock." She held it up for his review.

"Great," he muttered, wanting to shake her.

"Is it dead?"

"Yeah."

She used him as a post and pushed to her feet. He rose with her. Nick heard her bite back a low groan.

"Let me look at you." Nick checked her over. "Did the coyote bite you?"

"No." She stepped back from him.

He gave her a quelling glare. "You were too focused on being a damned heroine to notice if he'd taken a whole chunk out of you. What's wrong with your arm?"

She glanced down as if ashamed. "I think it's broken."

"Damn it all to hell."

"Watch your language."

"That was some shot," she said in admiring tones. "Right between me and the mare, and you still got him in one."

He ignored the compliment. Running his hands over her arms and legs, he looked for bites and scratches. Luckily, he didn't see any signs of damage, other than her arm. "I'll have to take you to the hospital."

His blood was still running high. Coming up the hill, he'd spotted the horse. He'd noticed how strange the rider was acting, but he hadn't seen the coyote until he'd pulled to a stop in the clearing. Then his heart had stood still.

He scooped Stephanie into his arms and headed for the truck.

"What are you doing?" she asked, obviously startled.

"Taking you to the truck. You're trembling."

"I can walk. You don't have to carry me."

Nick ignored her. "Is Doogie home? He needs to check your horse over real good. He can call the vet if he sees any marks or has questions."

"He's fishing at the river."

Nick muttered an expletive, then grunted when he heaved her into the truck. He went back for his rifle and the carcass.

After putting the coyote in a plastic bag, he tossed it in the back of the truck. The local officials would want to do an autopsy. They hadn't had a case of rabies in the county in years. The sheriff wouldn't be pleased to hear it.

Nick put the rifle into its scabbard behind the seat and drove off after checking that the mare was secure. Stephanie was holding her arm to her waist. Her face was pale.

"I can put a splint on that."

"That's okay," she said. "We're almost in town."

He called ahead. The emergency room staff was ready for them when they arrived. "Check her for bites or scratches." He followed the staff into a cubicle where the doctor had Stephanie sit on the side of the gurney.

"Did you get the coyote?" the doctor asked.

"In the truck. Shall I bring him in?"

"Take him to the morgue. I'll look at him later."

After giving the animal to the morgue attendant, Nick returned to the ER. "Coffee?" the nurse asked.

"Sure. She all right?"

"Mrs. Bolt? She has a hairline fracture in her wrist. She'll be fine, though. It won't take long to heal." She handed him a plastic cup filled with fresh coffee.

"Thanks." He took a sip. "You make the best coffee in town, Eileen. I'll give you a commendation for it if you ever need one."

"Maybe my future husband would be interested." She gave a little giggle that grated on his nerves.

"Hey, you getting married?" He checked the windows in the door marked No Admittance. He couldn't see Stephanie.

"Someday," the nurse said with a sigh. "I hope."

He realized she was looking at him in the way females do when they've got something on their minds. He pretended not to see it. "Uh, well, I'd better call this in to the sheriff. We'll put an alert out." He went to the truck to call instead of using the phone inside.

After talking to his boss, he called Stephanie's number. There was no answer. He left word for Doogie to get the mare if he got home before Nick brought Stephanie in, then added a quick explanation about the coyote.

When he returned to the emergency room, Stephanie was ready to go. She had a short, lightweight cast on her arm.

"I gave her a painkiller. She's woozy, so get her home and put her to bed. Here's a couple of pills in case she needs them later tonight," the doctor instructed. "She can eat anything she wants. Just don't let her move around a lot on her own."

"Right." He put his arm around her waist and guided her to the truck. She went without a word. In the truck she sighed and put her head back on the seat while he buckled her in. "I'll have to ask the doc what he gave you. For once that sharp tongue isn't stabbing holes in my ego."

"It's only temporary," she assured him.

He chuckled while he buckled himself in. In five minutes, he pulled into her drive. The house was dark and empty. Doogie wasn't back from his fishing expedition. Nick opened the back door and led Stephanie inside. He wasn't sure what to do.

"Supper," he said aloud, realizing he hadn't eaten. He placed Stephanie in a chair.

She spoke without opening her eyes. "There's soup in the refrigerator. I made it yesterday. It's vegetable with beef."

"Great. We'll eat, then get you to bed."

"I've eaten, but thank you, anyway," she declined politely.

He figured she didn't remember if she had or not. "Can you open your eyes?"

"It's too much trouble."

"That shot must have been pretty strong."

Her eyes opened. "Painkillers always affect me this way."

She shut them again.

Nick chuckled as he heated and served up two bowls of soup.

After eating—he had to prod Stephanie three times to keep her awake—he guided her into the bedroom she'd shared with Clay.

The other officer's picture was on the chest of drawers, as handsome as sin in his uniform, his smile wide and confident. Clay had been a lucky dude in more ways than one. The thought brought an unexpected pang.

Nick caught sight of his own features in the dresser mirror. Due to his bony face, women thought he was undernourished. They loved to feed him. He liked it, too, so that all worked out fine. Too bad Steph didn't have a soft spot for him. Once she'd thought he was wonderful. A long time ago. Before she'd forgotten him and married another man.

"What do you sleep in?" he asked. Sweat broke out on his brow. He ignored the heat gathering low in his body.

"A nightgown. Under the pillow."

Nick found it. When he shook it out, her scent drifted daintily from the folds. He wanted to bury his face in it, but refrained. "Let's get you tucked in. I think you're out for the night."

She nodded wearily. A strange tension swept over him.

Tenderness. Desire. Admiration for her courage. Fear for her life. He'd felt all those in the last two hours. He'd also seen her step between her horse and the coyote. In spite of her hurt arm, she'd held herself absolutely still while he drew a bead on the coyote.

Perspiration ran down his backbone while he unfastened her shirt. He fought an impulse to throw off his clothes and join her. As if he had the right.

Her hands lifted and settled on his. She opened her eyes. "I can do it," she said. "I'll call you when I'm ready."

He studied her. She looked steady enough. "Don't try to stand on your own. Call me when you're done."

"Help me to the bathroom."

He walked her over and left her at the door. He listened to the sounds inside, intimate sounds that only her husband had heard. He fought the useless anger left from his younger days when he'd thought he would be that husband....

When the door opened, he was there with his arm ready for her to lean on. She took it with a grateful smile. Her color was as pale as snowdrops against a snowbank. He circled her waist and half carried her to bed. When she was tucked in, the sheet safely over her pretty cotton nightgown with its girlish print of flowers on a blue background, he could breathe easy once more. Sort of.

Her eyes were closed again. She sighed, then stirred. Her eyes opened. "Thank you. You saved my life."

"No, you'd have beaten the poor ol' coyote to death with that rock. I just put him out of his misery a little faster."

She yawned and settled into sleep.

He stood there, watching her.

A noise in the kitchen drew him out of his contemplation of the woman he'd once loved. He returned to the kitchen.

"Mom?" Doogie turned from the sink. His eyebrows shot up when he saw who it was.

Nick put his finger to his lips. "She's asleep. There's been a slight accident." He filled the boy in.

Doogie listened, first stunned, then worried and finally proud as Nick told him Steph had protected her mount.

"Got a bed I can sleep in?" he asked when he finished.

Doogie looked relieved. "Yeah. We have a guest room."

"I'll take it."

While he helped Doogie stable the mare and finish the ranch chores, Nick wondered if he was borrowing trouble by getting involved in Steph's life. He *was* the county juvenile officer. He had a duty to keep an eye on her son.

Who was he trying to kid?

No, he wasn't there because of some honorable sense of duty. His feelings were much more primitive than that. Whether he wanted to admit it or not, he and Steph were involved. He wasn't sure how much or on what level, but the attraction was there. He'd seen it in her eyes when she'd gazed at him, tucked into bed and woozy from the shot. She'd known he was with her in her bedroom, watching her, wanting her....

Stephanie woke to a throbbing pain in her arm. Searching the floor beside the bed with her toes, she found her slippers and put them on. With her hurt arm hugged to her body, she went into the kitchen, vaguely recalling Nick laying the pain pills the doctor had given her on the windowsill over the sink.

Yes, they were there. The moonlight flooding the sill

reflected off the plastic wrap of the pills. She opened one and swallowed it down with a glass of water.

Lingering at the sink, she shivered as the cold night air circulated under her gown. The mountains surrounding the ranch loomed majestically over the meadows. Most of the cows and two of the horses were lying down. It was a peaceful scene.

At least, it used to be.

Now it appeared haunting in its loveliness, the mountains cold and remote, more like stern disciplinarians than the guardian angels she'd once thought they were.

The light flicked on. She whirled and found Nick standing at the door, gun in hand, his chest bare, his jeans on but unfastened. "Can't sleep?" he asked in conversational tones totally at odds with his appearance.

"No. That is, I woke with my arm hurting and remembered the pills in here. I'm ready to go back to bed."

"Umm." He walked around the room, peering out the windows, the gun now tucked into his pants, which he'd fastened. After his survey, he turned to her. "How about a cup of chocolate?"

"All right."

"I'll be right back." He left as suddenly as he'd appeared.

She poured milk into a pan, added cocoa and set it on the burner to heat. Nick returned with his socks and shirt on.

"That's right," she said sternly, "no shirt, no socks, no service." She giggled, then was surprised at herself.

Nick took a couple of mugs from their hooks and placed them on the counter. He stopped behind her and laid a hand on her waist. "Come sit down. I'll finish up." His voice was gruff, husky with sleep.

Old longings stirred in her, misty as moonlight on

mountain lakes, as old as the granite boulders on the ranch.

She sipped the cocoa and found it hot enough. "It's ready." She laid the spoon aside and turned the heat off. Then she did a strange thing. She leaned against Nick and closed her eyes.

His body heat slid over her, sending waves of warmth into the very center of her. It felt wonderful.

The pain in her arm eased, and she floated in a cloud, all silvery and shimmering inside, like the moonlight, only warm. Very warm.

His arms came around her, crossing at her waist and tucking her into the curve of his body as he bent over her. "You feel incredible," he murmured. His voice was thicker, softer.

He pushed her hair out of the way, then pressed his cheek to hers. It had been a long time since she'd felt the rasp of a man's beard against her face. He rubbed slowly, carefully, up and down, against her cheek.

The need to turn her head and touch him with her mouth rose in her. She wanted to explore him thoroughly.

Inhaling deeply, she drew in his scent. It filled her with the subtle essence of pure male—clean and masculine, infused with the musky undertone of human desire.

Pressing slightly, she felt the cold hardness of metal hit her back. She stiffened.

"Wait," he said and moved away. When he urged her against him again, the gun was gone, but the hardness wasn't. He rubbed her sides and along her waist, his long fingers spanning her abdomen. "I've thought of this. More and more of late."

"Have you?" Her voice came from a long way off, from some secret place inside. It urged her onward to some vague goal.

He pressed his face into her hair, his breath coming faster. "You always smell so good. I want to eat you up."

Shivers of unleashed desire danced like heat lightning all over her, through her scalp and skin, into her muscles, plunging layer by layer to the core of her body, making her hot, achy.

The years melted away. An eagerness for life trembled through her like a summer wind through aspen leaves. She felt young and so very vulnerable again.

This man was Nick, her first love. He was also the man who'd broken her heart into a thousand pieces that had taken weeks, months, years to heal.

"We shouldn't be doing this," she managed to whisper.

"Why?"

So many reasons whirled through her mind she couldn't name them, yet not one was clear or expressible. "Doogie—"

"Is asleep," he finished for her. "We're alone, Steph. Just you and me. Me," he repeated, "the man you once claimed to love. Is that the man you want, or will any man do?"

She shook her head. He'd always thought the worst of her, not bothering to ask for explanations when he'd found her with Clay. She'd needed him then, but he'd walked out, his angry accusations echoing in her heart long after he'd gone.

His hands held her captive when she would have moved from him. She was acutely aware of the passion that smoldered in him, of the hardness that ridged his jeans and pressed against her, reminding her of needs she'd locked away for two years.

She wanted...she wanted...she didn't know what she

wanted. Peace, perhaps. A contentment of the soul that had fled years ago. The trust that had been destroyed.

He turned her to face him, locking her in his embrace. She laid her hands on his chest, but didn't...couldn't... push him away. Belly touching belly, pelvis pressing pelvis, they stood and watched each other like enemies engaged in mortal battle.

But once he'd been her love.

His eyes were hot, cold, angry, hungry as he bent to her, his movements measured and controlled, as if she were a wild creature to be tamed to his will.

When his mouth touched the side of her face, she jerked a little. His hands rubbed over her back. He kissed her again, a butterfly stroke on the mole close to her mouth. He ran his tongue over it, exploring the tiny imperfection.

"I've wanted to do that again for years," he whispered in a hoarse drawl. "Years," he repeated and kissed her again, this time at the corner of her mouth. Then half her mouth. Then all.

She opened instinctively, wanting him inside. He followed her lead, not taking, not asking, just slowly consuming all of her in the kiss, drawing her closer, his tall, strong body moving against hers. Time became meaningless as the embrace continued.

At one point, briefly, she realized she'd locked her arms around his neck and was straining on tiptoe to have him closer. That was impossible. The only further intimacy was to shed their clothing and merge completely.

His hands stroked her back, her sides, her breasts. She drew a sharp breath, almost a sob.

"Yes," he encouraged. "Come apart for me, the way you used to, when we were both mindless with passion."

"I want..."

"Tell me," he murmured, lavishing kisses over her throat.

"What used to be."

He raised his head. His dark eyes glittered with something akin to outrage or hatred. "It can never be that way again. We can never go back to what we were before—"

Before I found you with another man was the rest of that statement.

She smoothed the dark lock that had fallen over his forehead. His hair was thick, its texture that of some crisp silky material. Its surface was cool, the underneath layers warm. She dropped her hand. "I didn't cheat on you, Nick."

He tightened his grip on her shoulders. "Don't lie, not after all these years."

"I'm not. You didn't trust me. You didn't believe in my innocence when I denied your accusations. I don't think I've ever quite forgiven you for that."

He reared back, his eyes glittering. "Why do I get the feeling I'm about to be put in the wrong even though I wasn't the one caught in another person's arms?"

"Maybe we were both wrong. You were too stubborn to call after you cooled down. I was too stubborn to try to explain. I always wondered—did you use my so-called betrayal as an excuse to break up? Some of my friends thought so."

His expression changed to outraged fury. "If you believed that, you didn't know me very well."

"Maybe not, but you didn't know me, either, if you thought I would cheat, then lie about it." The pain of those forgotten years rushed back into existence. She shook her head, trying to clear the muzziness caused by the pill from her head, trying not to say anything she'd regret later—

"Mom?" Doogie's call preceded him into the room.

Nick released her and stepped away. She turned blindly toward the stove and stirred the barely warm cocoa.

"In here," she called.

He entered the kitchen. "You all right?"

"Yes. I...my arm was hurting, so I took a pill. We're about to have some cocoa. You want some?"

"Sure." He sat at the table and hooked his heels on the chair rung. One sock was up, the other sagged around his ankle. He yawned and rubbed the sleep from his eyes.

Stephanie turned the heat back on under the pan and added more milk and chocolate. Nick set another mug on the counter.

She poured the steaming cocoa, added marshmallows and carried two mugs to the table. Nick brought his own and took a position across from Doogie. She sat in her usual place.

It was two o'clock in the morning.

A bewitching time. A time of weakness. She'd know to be careful of the night from now on, and to be on guard against her own uncertain control.

Physical pleasure wasn't enough. She'd learned that long ago when she'd needed him but he hadn't been available. She'd been alone after her father's death, studying and taking care of the small ranch. Clay had dropped in once in a while. To check on her, he'd said. But she'd seen the warmth in his eyes. She'd felt honor bound to tell him there was another. His kindness coupled with her loneliness had made her cry.

That's when Nick had arrived.

After they broke up, it had taken a long time for her to trust again. Clay had waited....

Nick sipped the hot drink, feeling the heat settle in his stomach. It didn't touch the cold spot inside him.

For a moment, he wondered if he'd been wrong all those years ago. It was hard to believe protestations of innocence after all this time. And it didn't matter a tinker's damn, anyway.

She didn't want the passion between them. He could see it in the way she refused to look at him, in the unnatural shade of her cheeks, in the emotions reflected in her eyes. Shame. Regret. Anger. He saw all those.

He didn't want the passion, either, but tell that to his libido. He mentally said all the expletives he could think of, but that did nothing to relieve the need to punch something. She drove him mad with equal parts desire and the urge to choke her.

"Is your arm hurting a lot?" Doogie asked. He licked a mustache of cocoa off his upper lip.

"Not now. The pill stopped the ache. I'd better get to bed. My eyelids are beginning to feel heavy."

"Right. Otherwise Nick and I will have to carry you. You were pretty much knocked out when I got in from fishing." He laughed with the delight of a child having the upper hand with his parent.

Nick watched her smile at her son. At one time she'd smiled at Nick in that natural, loving way—

Tearing his gaze from her, he automatically checked the windows, looking for movement in the darkness that would betray the presence of another. The yard and the pastures beyond it were peaceful. He could see the cows and horses bedded down in the bunch grass, their outlines discernible in the moonlight.

Doogie opened his mouth in a gaping yawn.

Stephanie took her cup to the sink. "You'd better head back to bed, too," she suggested.

"I will." But he stayed where he was. He took another

sip of cocoa, which was interesting since his cup was empty.

Nick said good-night to Stephanie, then watched her walk down the hall. He flicked his gaze back to Doogie and waited. He let the silence drone on while he kept his eyes on his cup. He took the last sip of his cocoa and pushed the cup away.

Doogie glanced down the hall, then back at Nick. "You knew my dad real well, didn't you?" he asked.

Nick felt a tightening in his gut. He hadn't expected Clay to be the subject of their conversation. "Yeah. He was my friend. We were partners for three years on the force."

"What if…what would you say if…what would you think if I told you he was a crook?"

Nick couldn't have been more surprised if Doogie had told him his dad was a serial killer. "Maybe you'd better tell me the whole story," he suggested.

"Two years ago, back before my dad died, I heard him talking to another man, arguing over something." Doogie linked his hands together on the table and clicked his thumbnails, something Clay used to do when he was stewing over something. "I think…I think they were talking about diamonds, only the other man called them rocks. He wanted to know where Dad hid them."

Nick nodded encouragement when Doogie stopped and looked at him with all the misery of a kid in a world gone wrong. The thought flicked through his mind that maybe Clay wasn't the hero Stephanie thought him to be. He was instantly ashamed of it.

"What did your father say?" Nick asked, keeping his voice neutral but reassuring.

Doogie shook his head. "They walked away from the barn—that's were I was—and went over to the guy's car, so I couldn't hear the rest. I...that was right after that summer place over on the lake was burglarized. Do you think Dad did it?''

"What brought this up now?" Nick asked. "Why are you worrying about it two years after the fact?"

Doogie's ears turned dull red. "I saw the guy Dad was talking to. He was in town—"

"When? Where?"

"At the Bear Tooth. He was standing on the sidewalk and looking down the street...at my mom. She was at the automated teller outside the bank."

A chill hit the back of Nick's scalp.

"That was about a month ago. I've seen him since, hanging around town, sort of not doing anything, you know?"

"Yeah. What did he look like?"

"Ordinary. About the same height and weight as my dad. He has a mole at his temple. Uh, the right one. It's black and has an irregular outline. He ought to get it checked. We studied skin cancer in health class last year."

Nick followed the odd turns and dips a kid's mind could take. His niece could cover three different subjects in one sentence and often did. He was used to it.

"When was the last time you noticed him in town?"

"Saturday. He was at the soccer game."

"I'll check him out," Nick promised.

"What do you think about Dad?"

Nick wanted to reach over and ruffle Doogie's bangs the way he did Nikki's and tell him not to worry, but he didn't, not in the face of that worried earnestness.

"I worked with your father for ten years. He was my partner for three of those years. There wasn't a straighter man alive. I'd stake my life on it. In fact, I did a couple of times. Remember when those two rustlers had me in a cross fire?''

Doogie nodded.

''Your dad took out the sniper who was about to do me in. He put his own life on the line to do it.'' He paused for emphasis. ''Clay Bolt was straight as an arrow.''

Doogie let out a breath as if he'd been holding it a long time. He got up abruptly and took his cup to the sink. Nick got a glimpse of the kid's face. The boy was close to tears and fighting it for all he was worth.

''Don't tell Mom,'' he said when he was under control again. ''She'd get mad because I sort of doubted Dad. She'd be hurt.''

A lump formed in Nick's throat. He had liked Stephanie's son before this, but now his respect grew tenfold. The boy had carried around a burden for two years, keeping it to himself to spare his mother's feelings. A man could be proud of a son like that.

He walked over and clamped a hand on Doogie's shoulder. ''We'll keep it to ourselves. I'll let you know what I find out about this other guy. If you see him in town, give me a call.''

''I will. Uh, will you tell me if you find out anything about Dad...like if something was wrong?''

''Yes.'' It was a promise. Doogie had a right to know the truth. Nick dropped his hand. ''What time do you get up to do the chores?''

''Six, usually.''

''We'd better get to bed. We have three hours to sleep before we have to get with it.''

''You don't have to help. I can do everything,'' Doogie protested, a pleased grin on his face.

''It's no problem. Next time I go out of town, I thought I would ask you to keep an eye on my place. I bought a few acres over on the East Creek across from your place. I keep llamas for some dude from Denver. Maybe you can help me figure out what the critters are good for."

"People use llama wool to make blankets and coats down in South America."

"Do they now?" Nick turned off the kitchen light and followed the boy into the hallway.

"Yeah. And llamas make good pack animals, too."

"Hmm, they could probably carry a sack of feathers. Did you know they can spit and hit a frog in the eye at fifty paces?"

"No, but they are kin to camels, I think."

"Yeah. One of 'em hit me in the middle of the forehead the first time I tried to check them for bloat flies. I was real tempted to find out what llama stew tasted like."

Doogie was still chuckling when he said good-night and went into his room. Nick went to bed but not to sleep. He couldn't make his mind turn off after the boy's story about Clay.

One thing for sure—he'd have to get to the bottom of the mystery or be haunted by it for the rest of his life.

Chapter Five

Stephanie woke to the sounds of masculine laughter. For a second, in the pause between one breath and another, she thought she'd awakened from a nightmare, that Clay was alive and well and the past two years had been a horrible dream.

"Breakfast," Doogie called outside her door. "Nick and I are going to eat it all if you don't get up, Mom."

Nick.

Shame washed over her. Last night...no, during the wee hours of the morning, she had let him touch her as no man ever had since Clay. And with her son in the house. Not that having Doogie out of the house would be an excuse for her behavior. No, such conduct was unacceptable. She would not allow herself to be swayed by Nick as she had when she'd been a girl.

"Be there in a minute," she called.

She would have to face Nick, but she'd be darned if she'd do it in her nightgown and robe. She washed up and dressed in slacks and an extra-large T-shirt, which went over her cast easily. After combing her hair and clipping it behind her ears, she decided against makeup. She didn't want Nick to think she was primping for him. Chin high, she ventured into the kitchen.

"Ta-da, surprise." Doogie gave her a big grin. There were plates of pancakes and bacon on the table.

She raised a hand to shield her eyes. "Please, your smile is blinding this early in the morning."

His laughter cracked from a low G to a middle E, reminding her again of his pending adult status. The thought brought tears to her eyes. She hid them behind the glass of orange juice Doogie pressed into her hand.

"Good morning."

Nick's greeting forced her to look at him. He wore the jeans and shirt from yesterday. He had his shoes and socks on this morning. The gun wasn't in sight.

"Hello." She feigned surprise. "I thought you'd be on duty, patrolling the highway for speeding cows or something."

"I'm off today."

"He helped me with the chores, Mom. We already have everything done."

"That was very nice." What else could she say? Her son's glances at the deputy were filled with admiration.

The bleak despair that had overcome her after Clay's death threatened her determined cheer. She swallowed a gulp of juice and choked. It took a moment of coughing and gasping to get things working right again.

"You okay?" Nick asked. His eyes pierced through her defensive armor, knowing more of her than was his right.

"Of course. I just swallowed wrong." She took her place at the table. The two males sat at either side of her. Clay used to sit across from her. He liked to look up and see her, he'd always said.

That wasn't true for their guest. Nick didn't seem to like anything about her this morning. He was certainly hard to figure out. Last night…last night had been a moment of mindless need. She wouldn't let herself need anyone that way ever again.

"Can I, Mom?" Doogie scooped up the last bite of pancake and stuffed it in his mouth.

"I'm sorry. What did you say?"

He swallowed and wiped his mouth. "Clyde and I are gonna ride over to Nick's place and look at his llamas. He said it was all right." This last was spoken defensively.

"Oh. Well, I suppose. When are you going?" She glanced over at her unwanted guest.

His smile was lazy, mocking her eagerness to get rid of him. "The boys can go over after breakfast. I volunteered to do the dishes."

"You don't have to. I can manage."

"Nope, this is your day to rest," he stated.

She recognized the determination in his manner. A sinking sensation attacked her middle. He obviously wanted to talk to her about last night. Perhaps they should get it out into the open. She needed to tell him it wouldn't happen again. She'd been so careful of her reputation. She didn't want to ever give Doogie reason to be embarrassed by her actions as she and her father had been when her mother had left them.

She paused and faced the truth squarely. She was afraid of the attraction between her and Nick.

Clyde arrived before she finished the meal. Doogie asked to be excused and took off like a goose who hears the call of the wild. A somber silence fell on the ranch after the clatter of hooves died away in the distance.

"Ah, to be young again," Nick remarked. He pushed

his plate aside and settled back with his coffee mug resting on his stomach. He rubbed a finger around the thick, curved handle.

His hands had been gentle when he'd caressed her. His touch had been...exquisite. A flush rose to her face, composed of equal parts passion and regret. She put a hand to her forehead, hiding her eyes from his steady perusal.

Coward. She simply couldn't look him in the eye this morning. Not after acting the wanton last night. As painful as it was to admit, she had been the one who'd started that torrid session by leaning into him.

"Is your head hurting?" he asked. "There's another pill—"

"No, no, I'm fine." She lifted her head and smiled. She even looked him in the eye. A mistake. The expression in those depths caused a tremble to quake through her. It wasn't fair for a man to look so...so concerned.

"Stephanie."

The sound of her name on his lips had her clenching her good hand in her lap. Her injured arm throbbed as the blood pounded heavily through her body. "Yes?"

"We need to talk."

There was no avoiding it. She'd known they'd have to discuss that long, passionate interlude sometime. Nick wasn't the type to let anything drop. Clay had said he was one of the best investigative officers on the force, that he was like a bulldog—once he got his teeth in something, he didn't let go until he had it all figured out. She resisted the need to hide her face. "Yes."

"Doogie and I had a chat after you went to bed last night."

Oh, no, had her son seen them? How would she ever explain it to him when she couldn't explain it to herself?

"He's worried about Clay. He overheard his father and another man talking— What is it?"

She closed her mouth with an effort. "You want to talk about Doogie and his father?" she asked in weak tones.

"Yes." His eyes lit with bitter amusement. "Would you rather talk about last night first?"

"No." She almost threw the word at him. "What... what about Doogie and Clay?"

Nick grew serious. "The boy thinks his father may have been mixed up in something crooked. He heard Clay and another man arguing about some rocks after that robbery over at the lake. He thinks they were talking about the diamond necklace that wasn't recovered after the theft."

For the briefest instant, she wondered if perhaps that was why Clay had been moody and remote that summer. He'd been quick to anger and not at all his usual easygoing self.

She stared down at her clasped hands. Or perhaps she was looking for something to excuse her own temper that morning he'd left the house earlier than usual and was killed. She'd been so angry with him. He hadn't understood her need to do something other than take care of him and Doogie. She was more her mother's daughter than she wanted to admit.

She forced herself to face Nick. "Doogie thinks Clay had something to do with it?"

He nodded. "He asked me if I thought his father was a crook."

She pressed the back of her hand to her mouth. "What...what did you say?"

His eyes narrowed. He studied her a second before answering. "That I'd check into it."

"There's nothing to check. Clay was as honest as... He would never do anything wrong."

"Umm," Nick said.

"Do you doubt him?" she demanded, furious.

"No, but you did for a minute. Why?"

"No, I..." Her protest died in her throat.

"Why, Steph?" he persisted. "What did you know or what did you suspect that made you think Clay could be guilty?"

"Nothing!" She leapt from her chair. "Quit trying to put words in my mouth. Clay was wonderful. A wonderful father. A wonderful husband. A wonderful man." She reined in the torrent of protest. "He was proud of his job on the force. He would never do anything to disgrace his uniform."

Silence filled the kitchen. She could hear her breathing, a raspy, angry sound. She forced herself to inhale deeply and let it out slowly, once, then twice.

Nick continued to study her as if she was the prime suspect in one of his cases.

"He wouldn't," she added in a calmer tone. "Never." She went to the coffee maker and filled her cup. Not that she could get it past her throat. She needed to get away from Nick's gaze.

"I know that." His chair scraped the floor as he stood. "But Doogie needs to understand what he heard. I need to find out who the man was. Doogie says he's back in town. And watching you."

She faced him. "Watching me?"

Nick inclined his head.

"Could there be some danger to Doogie?"

"I don't know." He shoved aside the lock of hair that jutted over his forehead. It sprang back into position.

She recalled the exact texture of those silky strands, the

stubbornness of the cowlick, the coolness hiding the warmth underneath those thick tresses. Her palm tingled as heat swept down her hand. She gazed at it blindly.

"I'll keep an eye on both of you," Nick told her. He picked up the dishes and began cleaning the kitchen.

"Don't," she said. "You don't have to keep an eye on me. I'm sure there's no danger...." Looking into Nick's eyes, she wasn't sure of that at all.

He gave her an intent stare. "When I'm sure of that, I'll let you know. And then we'll talk about us."

"There is no us."

"There was once. What happened to that couple, Steph? That was one thing I never figured out."

"You know what happened. You caught me in the arms of another man. You said there was nothing I could say to change the facts. As you saw them, Nick. As you interpreted them."

The hurt and anger of his distrust swept over her as if it had been yesterday.

"According to you, I was wrong in that interpretation."

She couldn't tell if he was being cynical or not. "Yes."

He nodded once, then finished his chore. After slamming the dishwasher closed, he walked out the door. Without another word. Without another glance.

She sank into her chair, rattled by the encounter without knowing why. Unanswered questions and arguments whirled though her mind.

She didn't know how long she sat there, her thoughts in a turmoil. Their mutual past had no place in their future. She had a son to raise and a business to run so she could make a living for that son. She had no time for foolishness left over from their youth. That's what she had to tell him.

Nick mentally checked the description Doogie had given him. About Clay's height and build. And a mole on the temple. Yes, it was there. The guy was dressed in jeans, a long-sleeved work shirt, and scuffed hiking boots. He looked like any cowboy or logger from the area. Or any tourist, for that matter.

Sitting in his cruiser, Nick watched the man who was watching Stephanie.

He flicked a glance her way. She was an easy target if someone had it in mind to off her. Standing in the window of the boutique in her bare feet, she was bathed in morning sunshine, her every movement visible from either direction on the street.

She had no idea she was being watched. So much for her avowal she didn't need looking after. She was totally focused on the mannequin she was outfitting in a hunter green suit that looked a mite warm for July, even in the mountains.

He thought of how she would look in the outfit. He'd take her up to the ski lodge for dinner. She'd be wearing the suit. When they returned to her place, she'd invite him in. She'd take off the jacket. Later, in front of the fire, he'd take off the silk blouse and the green skirt. Then—

With a curse, he realized his quarry had disappeared. While he'd been daydreaming about something that would never happen, the man had vanished. He muttered an expletive.

Swinging down from the truck, he walked toward Stephanie's place. At that moment the guy walked out of the video store.

Nick stopped by a car whose parking meter had expired and wrote out a ticket. His quarry gave him a glance, then hurried down the street in the opposite direction. Nick grinned. It would be ironic if the vehicle he was ticketing belonged to the guy. After sticking the ticket under the windshield wiper, he ambled over to the video place.

"Do you know the guy who was just in here?" he asked after greeting Joe Moss, the owner.

Joe shook his head. "He's been in a couple of times. Rented a video the other day."

"Got a name and address?"

"Yeah. Hold on while I look it up." He clicked through the computer files, then put on a pair of glasses and searched through the list of customers. "He in trouble?"

"Nah. I've seen him around town lately. He doesn't seem to have a job. I need some help on my place."

"Here he is. Bob Greenwood. Lives in that boarding house over on East Madison."

"Thanks. I'll look him up."

"You need a set of prints?" Joe gave him a sly glance. "He picked up this new video on display here. Made the wife mad. She'd just dusted 'em and put 'em in order."

Nick took out a handkerchief. "Got a bag?"

"Sure thing."

The store owner held a plastic bag while Nick put the video inside. "I'll sign for it."

"No need. I'll trust you to bring it back."

"Thanks. I owe you one." Nick exchanged a look of understanding with Joe. When he left, he heard Joe tell his wife the deputy was inquiring about a hired hand. He didn't mention the video or fingerprints.

At the station Nick went to the crime lab. It was nothing like the one at the police academy where he'd taken his forensic training, but it was adequate. He lifted the prints himself and put in the order for a computer check through the FBI files. After returning the video to the store, he went out on patrol.

Stephanie, he noticed, was still arranging the display in

the shop window. Kneeling, her feet bare, she busily tangled scarves in a pile as if they'd been casually blown there by the wind, like autumn leaves.

Once she had run laughing through the woods with him. They'd fallen into the thick pile of leaves beneath a tree, and there he'd kissed her for the first time. He grimly brought his mind back to the present.

After finishing his tour of duty, Nick headed for town. At the office he found the computer printout from the FBI on his desk. "Damn," he exclaimed softly upon reading over the information on Bob Greenwood.

The guy Doogie had seen two years ago, the same guy who was back and watching Steph, wasn't Bob Greenwood. His name was Bob Greesley. He used to be a cop—a cop who'd gone bad.

According to the FBI files, Greesley had been an L.A. Vice Squad detective for sixteen years. He'd gone to prison for stealing evidence—boats, cars, jewelry—and selling it.

Nick's first thought upon reading the sheet was of Steph and Doogie and their safety. A fierceness rose in him, a need to protect those that belonged to him—

He put a brake on the thought. Neither Steph nor her son belonged to him. His duty was to all the citizens of the county. Steph and Doogie were two of them, no more, no less.

He spoke to the sheriff. "Doogie Bolt thinks his dad was mixed up in something. Was Clay working on that diamond job, the summer house break-in during that series of robberies a couple of years back?"

The sheriff shook his head. "That was Barkley. However, there is an interesting link. Clay went to the police academy in California. He worked two years at the LAPD before moving back here when his dad died. That would have been during the time Greesley was on the force.''

Nick frowned. "Do you think there's a connection?''

The sheriff's smile was grim. "I don't know. What I do want to know is what Greesley is doing here now and what he was doing here two years ago.''

"I'd like access to Clay's records, his daily sheets, reports, things like that. If there was something going on, I'll find it. Greesley's timing fits. As a cop, he'd know that by the end of two years, the heat would be off.''

"Yeah, with Barkley retired and gone to Texas, there's no one here who's familiar with it." The sheriff pulled on his lower lip while he thought it over. He reached for the phone. "I'll tell records you're to have access.''

"Would you mind letting me pull my own stuff? I would rather no one knew what I'm checking on.''

"That might be a good idea. If we have bad apples in the department, I want to find them. Can you cover it with your regular work, or do I need to find some excuse for you to hang around town?''

"I can handle it.''

"Good. By the way, the mayor is really pleased about your youth program. Vandalism and petty theft are down over forty percent since you started the soccer team and got the swim club going. Good work." The telephone rang. The sheriff glared at it, then picked it up and waved as Nick left the office.

Nick was satisfied with his assignment. As the special investigator on the case, he could delve into the problem of Clay and his possibly shady past with official sanction, and he damned well wanted to know everything there was to know about Bob Greesley, the ex-cop and ex-con, who called himself Greenwood.

He cruised until nearly three, then drove to town and

picked up Doogie for soccer practice. On the way to the field, he called in and signed out for the day.

"You like your job?" Doogie asked.

"Yeah."

"How did you decide to be a cop, uh, an officer."

"I don't mind being called a cop. How did I decide on being one? Well, I always wanted to wear a uniform, and I was too short for basketball, too light for football and the army didn't need anyone."

Doogie grinned. "My dad said he thought cops got a bad rap. He wanted to be one of the good ones, the ones that people trusted and...and everything." His voice broke before he finished. A flush spread into his face.

Nick felt the kid's distress. He warred with his conscience for all of five seconds. "Listen, I'm checking into the situation you told me about, an official investigation. The sheriff okayed it. This is between you and me, you understand?"

"Yeah, sure." Doogie grabbed his shin guards when the truck stopped. "Hey, that's great. You will tell me if..." His voice trailed off, and he gave Nick an uncertain glance.

"I said I would."

They went to join the rest of the team on the field. Nick couldn't help but feel a proprietary interest in Doogie. The kid was a good player—smart, capable and generous with his teammates—the kind of son a man would be proud to claim.

Doogie had been named after his father—Clayton Douglas Bolt, Jr., Nick recalled. For a second, bitterness stung his tongue like an acid bath before he pushed aside the thought that Steph's kids should have also been his.

He sat on the bench while the team divided up and played a game against each other. Looking at their young, energetic bodies, listening to their boisterous shouts and friendly insults, he was acutely aware that he was twenty years older than most of them.

Thirty-four. Thirty-five before Christmas. Lately he'd been feeling his age. Not that he felt old. Only that life was passing him by. He knew what he wanted. He'd known for a long time. Wife. Home. Family. He'd envied Clay.

It was hell to want a woman who was married to another man, especially when that man was your friend. Worse still was feeling she should have been his. A fury arose that only thoughts of Steph could induce. He shook it off.

Whatever she'd felt for him had died. After that quarrel, the only serious one they'd ever had, she'd not written or called him once. He'd dated a lot the next year…to show her he was over her and that stinging betrayal, which she now insisted wasn't a betrayal at all.

A few years ago he'd planned to marry and have a family, but that had fizzled out. His fiancée had said he didn't really love her, not as she needed to be loved. She'd said she couldn't fight a ghost. She had known he and Steph had been a couple at one time. He couldn't obliterate the past, but he certainly wasn't still in love with Steph, nor was she with him.

His gaze swung back to Doogie. The boy was living proof there was nothing between them. That was a fact. Steph's child wasn't his. But she'd been his first love.

Get over it, he advised himself with cynical disregard for the young man he'd once been.

The attraction was still there. He hadn't imagined that. It made him angry, this adolescent need that wouldn't go away, that lingered like a festering thorn he couldn't remove.

If he were smart, he'd be searching for a woman who'd love him until the end of time. Yeah, right. Well, he had to finish this case. He would clear Clay's name for the boy's sake. And Steph's, too. Then he would be history. He'd been thinking of leaving the area for a long time. Maybe it was time to move on.

"Hey, Coach, did you see that pass? Was it outside or not?"

"Sorry, guys, you'll have to decide."

"Is that taking the easy way out?" a feminine voice asked.

He whirled around, his heart speeding up. Stephanie stood in front of him in a cream silk shirt and navy slacks, looking as sleek as an otter, as distant as a dream.

Stephanie pushed a strand of hair behind her ear. She watched Nick's gaze run over her and was disappointed when he looked away as if uninterested. Not that she wanted to attract him, just the opposite, in fact. She hesitated, wondering if that were true. His kiss had lingered on her lips and in her mind since that night at the ranch.

"Hello, Nick." She sat on the bench.

"Hi. You might get your slacks dirty," he warned.

"They're washable."

"Hmm." He kept his eyes on the game.

She watched the boys play for a few minutes. "Soccer involves a lot of running. No wonder Doogie eats like he's been on a starvation diet for months these days."

"He's a good player," Nick said. "All the guys put a lot into the game."

"I can see that."

"So what brings you out?"

She rubbed her right hand over the cast. Her wrist ached today. "I haven't been able to get away more than an hour at a time on Saturdays to see the games. I thought

I'd catch a practice session and check with you to see how Doogie is doing.''

Brutal honesty forced her to admit this man might have also had something to do with her being here. She couldn't stop thinking about him and that angry, hungry kiss they'd shared.

"Hmm."

"You were right," she said softly. "Doogie did need to be with boys his own age. The sport has been good for him."

He cut his dark eyes in her direction. "Well, well," he said sardonically, "was that an admission of error, or do my ears deceive me?"

"I'm trying to eat crow gracefully," she told him. She didn't sound gracious at all, more like a shrew.

He raised his eyebrows in mock surprise. "Sorry, I didn't know that's what you were doing. I usually eat mine with a lot of bluster and denial of doing anything of the sort."

Underneath the cynical humor, she sensed the currents that flowed bitter and tense between them. For some reason it made her sad. Once they'd been close, friends as well as lovers.

"Can't we be friends?" she asked.

She felt him stiffen, and risked a quick glance his way. His angular jaw was set and his expression was one of disgust.

"For Doogie's sake," she added, hating the defensiveness she heard in her voice. She had nothing to be defensive about, for heaven's sake. Nick always threw her off balance.

"No," he said softly, angrily. "Hell, no. That's not enough, Steph. You know it."

"Please." She didn't want the boys to hear them arguing. Doogie thought Nick could do no wrong. If he'd seen that kiss in the kitchen—

She shied from the memory. It haunted her—the way his eyes had burned over her, the way his hands had caressed her. The memory caused her breath to catch in her throat and her stomach to tie itself into knots.

"Please what?" he demanded in a low, harsh voice. "Don't want you? Tell me how to stop. God knows I don't need this. My life is complicated enough as it is. Tell me how to forget what was once between us. Or was it all on my part? Was I living in a fool's paradise?"

She pressed a hand to her lips, remembering the wild kisses they had once shared, the way her heart had beaten madly whenever she saw him, the passion she'd always felt with him. She shook her head helplessly.

"You responded all those years ago and last week, too. That's what I remember. I thought you loved me. I seem to recall those words somewhere in our youthful conversations. Love and marriage. A future. That what I heard. Tell me what your memories are, Steph, and we'll compare notes."

"Nick, don't," she begged. "You're right. Our lives are complicated enough. If we can't be friends..." She hesitated to add that they couldn't be lovers. Not ever again.

"Maybe we'll be lovers. Maybe not. But we won't be friends. That's the way it has to be," he said.

She stared at him, shocked at the bitterness in his tone as much as the words. There were other emotions present, but she didn't know what they were. He turned his head and looked her in the eye. Then he smiled.

Well, maybe it was more of a wry grimace, but it looked kinder than his earlier scowl. She breathed a sigh of relief. "I thought you were serious there for a minute."

"I never joke about things like that."

Her heart lurched around crazily. "I don't understand," she whispered. "I don't understand any of this."

"Which part isn't clear?" he asked on a facetious note. "The part about being friends? Or is it being lovers that puts worry in your eyes? There was a time when you came to me as eager as a pup for a romp."

"We were hardly more than children," she informed him, her back going stiff.

"You didn't feel like a child in my arms. You were all woman, Steph, a warm and willing woman. My woman."

"Yours, Nick?" she demanded, angry at his possessive tone.

"It worked both ways," he assured her with an arrogant tilt to his chin. "I belonged to you, too. Yours, Steph, for the taking—all my heart's dreams, everything I had or was. But never again. We're both older and wiser. This time we don't have to coat passion in pretty words."

He stood and whistled between his fingers. The boys completed the play, then started for the bench. Doogie grabbed the ball and carried it, twirling it on one finger, toward them.

Stephanie sat there stunned while Nick went over the things each of the guys needed to work on, then sent them home. He lifted one finger to his forehead toward her, then climbed in his truck and left, too.

"Hey, Mom, what are you doing here?" Doogie asked, stopping in front of the bench.

"I'm not sure," she answered truthfully, feeling as if she'd fallen over an unseen cliff. She pulled her ragged composure together. "Actually I came to see how you were doing, since I've only seen bits and pieces of the real games. I'm sorry about that, Doogie."

An expression of pleased surprise ran over his face. "That's okay. It's no big thing."

"It is to me. I'll see the next game in its entirety if I have to throw the customers out and close the shop." She gave her son a mock-ferocious frown before smiling. "How about a pizza tonight?"

"Hey, all right!" His laughter floated on the warm evening air as they ambled to the car for the drive home.

She relaxed during the trip and listened to her son expound on their chances of making the county finals in soccer. Life was easy between them now. Things were working out. Once she got over this ridiculous situation with Nick, her life would be fine.

Chapter Six

"When did he leave?" Nick swore silently, but kept his face bland while waiting for the boardinghouse owner to answer.

She had the round face and dark eyes of her Italian ancestors. This woman's mother and his grandmother had come from the same mountain village over seventy years ago.

"He said he had a job on a ranch. He didn't say where, but he drove off toward the west."

"Looks like I missed out. I wanted some help on my place for the summer. Well, I'd better get back on patrol. Don't tell the sheriff I was here." He grinned, thrust his hair back and jammed his hat on before the cowlick could flop back over his forehead.

"I won't." She laughed at their secret and walked to the end of the porch with him.

Nick cursed again as he drove off. His quarry was as elusive as an eel. He cursed his own carelessness that had let the dude slip out of his clutches, so to speak. He had a vehicle description—a black pickup. Probably no more than half the guys in the state drove black pickups.

In town he appeared in court in a domestic violence case. This time the woman testified against her husband...after the man had nearly beaten her to death.

When he'd been younger and still idealistic, he'd once asked Clay why women put up with men. The older cop had laughed. "Whose side are you on?" he'd asked.

"The right side," he'd answered. "No one has a right to hit another person."

"Didn't your dad ever wallop you when you were growing up?"

"Yeah. I'll never do that to my kids."

Clay had thought that funny, too. "Me, either, but you'll sure as hell feel like it."

At the rate he was hurtling toward marriage and family, Nick figured he'd never have a chance to find out. He left the courthouse feeling low and cynical. The first person he saw was Stephanie, going into the Bear Tooth with a suave dude in a pinstripe suit. Ah, yes, the new attorney in town. The city slicker had wasted no time in finding the prettiest woman in the county.

It was all he needed to finish off the day. In this mood he cruised the highway, gave out twenty tickets for speeding and three warnings for brake lights and turn signals being out. He headed for the ranch when his tour of duty was over.

The primitive cabin on the property had seemed good enough for the nights he stayed there. Now it looked like what it was—a line shack left over from the days when cowboys rode herd and checked fences on one of the biggest spreads in these parts. When the old rancher had died, his kids had sold the ranch in parcels and shipped their mom to a nursing home.

Maybe he should build a house, a real one with indoor plumbing and the works. "Whadda ya say?" he asked the llamas who stuck their heads over the fence when he arrived.

Their gazes were bright and inquisitive. They looked more intelligent than they actually were. Like some others he could mention. Such as himself. Pining for a woman...

"Ah, hell," he muttered, angry for the things he'd said earlier, for letting his temper override his common sense.

He watched the twilight deepen the sky to dark blue, reminding him of Steph's eyes as they sometimes looked when she was troubled. Not that her troubles were any of his business, as she'd made clear.

Gritting his teeth, he waited for the spasm of pain that hit him to subside. All week he'd been seized with yearning that was a tangle of old and new needs.

A man who didn't learn from his past mistakes was a fool and deserved all he got, he reminded himself.

The llama that liked to spit took aim. He saw it coming in time and sidestepped. "That's two for me and one for you, buddy. You hit me again and you're llama stew."

Stephanie patted the calf and pushed its head away when it would have grabbed the end of her shirt and sucked on it.

"Spoiled, you are," she scolded when it bawled at her. She rinsed out the bucket in the barn and set it on the shelf.

One of the barn cats wrapped itself around her legs. She stooped and gave its ears a scratching. It closed its eyes and purred in ecstasy. If only other things in life were as easy and simple to please as this, she mused.

She went inside and ate a solitary dinner. Doogie was sleeping over at Clyde's house. The boys were great friends again. Clyde was on the soccer team, too. They both quoted their coach often and as the ultimate authority.

The night air was chilly when she went outside to sit on the porch. She'd showered and put on sweats and thick socks, but couldn't settle down to read. She was so restless lately. Since Nick had kissed her. She closed her eyes, but couldn't get rid of the image or the feel of his mouth on hers, coaxing a response in spite of her better sense.

She tried to think of other things, such as staying on the small ranch. Winters were hard out here. Perhaps she and Doogie would be better off living in town.

The quiet bothered her. With the lights out in the house, the homestead seemed deserted. The moon was still bright, though, shining on the meadow with a silvery glow. She pressed her right hand to her heart, which ached unbearably.

Her injured wrist throbbed in sympathy. She rubbed above and below the cast to ease the pain. She'd unpacked merchandise every spare minute of the day and had probably overused it.

With no warning, tears gathered behind her eyes. She laid her head on her knees and wept for things she couldn't name, for a life that would never be again, for the love that was gone.

Nick's image appeared in her inner vision.

For a moment she didn't know which love she meant. She went to bed still feeling weepy.

The sun wasn't up when Stephanie woke. Her head was stuffy and her throat ached. A summer cold, she diagnosed. She slid into her slippers and washed up before going to the kitchen to put on a pot of coffee. She decided to forego church that morning. She'd paint the trim on the barn instead.

Going out to get the paper, she noticed the rear end of a truck parked behind the stable. Curious, she walked over to the barn and quietly walked along the side of it.

Peering around the corner, she spied a man nosing around the stable that had once housed Morgan horses when this section had been part of a large ranch. The door was open, and she could see him poking into boxes stored on the shelves. He moved out of sight toward the stalls against the back walls.

The tips she'd picked up as a cop's wife came to her. She needed to get something to pin an ID on. His license plate would do. She slipped across the open space between the barn and the stable. Soundless in her slippers, she headed for the back of the truck.

Upon reaching the corner of the stable, she realized the man had opened the double bay doors on that end. Or maybe she or Doogie had left them open. At any rate, she couldn't get past them to the truck without being seen.

Maybe she should slip back into the house and call Nick. While she pondered the situation, she heard a noise inside the stable. The man came outside and began closing the doors.

She knew she'd been spotted, but he was pretending she wasn't standing in plain sight. A cold hand of fear caressed her neck. Sometimes offense was the best defense.

"Can I help you?" she asked, deliberately hostile, but not excessively. She put a note of curiosity in the question.

The cowboy whirled around, his eyes wide, then narrowing as he checked her over. He smiled. "Well, the boss told me to check for some branding irons over this way, but I didn't think anyone lived here anymore." He appeared somewhat confused.

"This is my place you're on. Who told you to come here?"

He pushed his hat back and looked around. "I just hired on over at the Double Bar S. This isn't their place?"

"No. The fence is the dividing line."

"There was a gate," he admitted. "The padlock was rusted and broken. Sure am sorry about intruding, ma'am. I hope I didn't scare you." His dark eyes ran over her sweats, which she had worn to bed.

His drawl was a fair imitation of John Wayne, but not good enough to fool her into thinking he was for real.

She forced a smile. "My land starts at the creek and runs to the road. Sixty acres. I have twenty cows and three horses, a few cats and a dog that's at the vet's." This last was a lie, but she'd get a dog tomorrow.

He glanced around. "Neat little spread. Well, I'd better find that barn I was told to check."

"Across the creek and to the south about a mile. That's where they load their cattle. You'll see the chute."

"Thanks." He tipped his hat and headed for his truck.

She noticed he backed in a wide circle, preventing her from getting a close look at his license number. However she had keen sight. After he drove off, she picked up a pebble and scratched the number into the dirt. Then she went to call Nick.

He arrived in five minutes.

"Come on in," she called when he came to the kitchen door. He took off his hat and entered. "Pancakes?"

He looked her over and heaved a deep breath. "I was afraid I'd find you murdered or something."

A flutter riffled her heart at his concern, before she recalled his words from the day before and got herself under control. "I told the dispatcher I was fine." She frowned with apprehension. "You said Doogie told you there was a guy watching me. I didn't believe you."

"But you do now?" He hung his hat on a free hook by the door and took a seat at the oak table.

"Some cowboy was over here poking around in the stable. He pretended to be on the wrong property when I asked him what he was doing. I think he was lying."

"Naturally you had to barge outside and accost him," Nick said in a disgusted tone.

"I was already outside when I saw his truck. Actually I was trying to get his license number. He must have seen me through the cracks in the stable slats."

"Did you get the number?"

"Yes, but it was a ranch truck. He said he'd just signed on at the next spread." She handed him a memo with the number.

He studied it, then stuck the slip in his pocket. "What did he look like?"

She described the man.

"That's him," Nick said. "The same man I saw last week when I was watching you."

She whirled on him. "You were watching me?"

"Yeah, I told you I'd keep an eye out. You were arranging the window at the shop." His smile mocked her. "You wouldn't have known if an army had been watching."

"I'd hardly be in any danger in the shop window."

"Maybe. Maybe not. How about a cup of coffee? I turned the pot off before it boiled and hightailed it over here when I got the call."

She poured the coffee and set two mugs on the table.

He picked his up and took a drink. "Ah, the stuff of life. The dispatcher said you asked for me."

"You were the one who warned me."

"Yeah, but you could have taken whoever was on duty." His gaze challenged her to deny it.

"You usually have this area."

"I was off today."

"Oh." She hadn't considered that. "I really didn't think about it at all," she said coolly.

His face hardened.

She couldn't think of anything to add that wouldn't put them on the dangerous ground of yesterday. After taking up the last pancake, she carried the plates to the table and brought silverware over. "I'm worried about Doogie. If this person knows my son can identify him, he might try something."

Nick waited for her to sit, his gaze taking in her shorts and the blouse tied at her middle, her hair hooked behind her ears. She looked eighteen again, which was about the age he felt around her. "I think I might move over here."

She shook her head. "I'm going to get a dog."

He couldn't suppress a wry chuckle. "Nice to know I can be replaced so easily."

Her mouth crimped at the corners and pursed up in the middle as if she was annoyed. He suppressed a desire to lean across the corner of the table and kiss the starch out of her. That would be a serious mistake. He might not be able to stop.

"I meant, to let me know when someone comes around here."

"Then what will you do, beat 'em with a rock the way you intended to do with the coyote?"

"I have Clay's forty-four. By the way, the coyote wasn't rabid. The coroner's office called me."

"Yeah, I read the report. It was some kind of poison. They've sent the carcass to the state lab to try to identify it. Probably a rancher mixed up his own concoction and put it out.''

She ate without comment for a few minutes. ''Your work is never done, is it? If it isn't crooks or suspicious characters, it's the locals doing their thing without regard to the law.''

Her sympathy was a soothing balm. However, it wasn't exactly what he wanted from her. So what did he want?

He frowned as he thought it over. He wouldn't let himself think a few kisses meant forever the way he had all those years ago. A man took life the way it was, not as he dreamed it might be. He would not get lost in passion once again with her.

''What is it?'' she asked as if sensing his thoughts.

He met her curious gaze with a guarded one of his own. ''Nothing. By the way, I *am* moving in.''

Stephanie smoothed a strand of hair behind her ear, not sure she'd heard right.

He ate his breakfast as if this were an ordinary day in their lives. It occurred to her that they had been having entirely too many meals together of late, three or four in the past couple of weeks. She wished she hadn't offered him a cup of coffee, much less pancakes and sausage.

''What did you say?''

''You heard me.'' He glanced up with an amused smile on his face, but his gaze was hard and uncompromising.

She decided to ignore his surly humor. She'd often found that had been the best approach whenever she and Clay had disagreed. She would wait him out. She gave him a stare that was usually effective with the men in her life. It clearly expected them to do things her way. With Nick, the tactic didn't work.

''I'm going to move in with you and Doogie for a

while. To keep an eye on things. You won't have to get a dog."

His grin was sarcastic, slightly skewed to the right and supremely confident. It annoyed her.

"You certainly are not."

"Umm-hmm," he contradicted softly. "I'm working on a case. You're a lead in solving it. I can get a court order to move in, but it would be better if you cooperated, easier all the way around, don't you think?"

"For me or for you?" Her tone dripped sarcasm, which he appeared not to notice.

She made her gaze as blistering hot as she could when next he looked up. He returned it, his expression arrogantly sure that his decision was the right one.

Then she noticed his eyes held the fiercest, most ruthless expression she'd ever witnessed. She recoiled slightly, not out of fear—she knew he wouldn't hurt her—but because she'd never seen him like this.

Warrior.

The word came to her unbidden and had nothing to do with his being a deputy. It was more primitive than that, more subtle, imprinted deeply into the genetic material of his being, a part of him as much as being right-handed.

"For both of us." He jabbed his fork at the air for emphasis. "You can be stubborn and make life difficult, or you can cooperate. Either way, the result will be the same."

She felt herself growing stubborn, just as he said. She could feel the corners of her mouth crimping in, the way Doogie's did when he was angry. Nick watched her without comment.

His gaze settled on the mole at the side of her mouth, then switched to her lips. She patted them self-consciously with her napkin. Slowly the fierceness in his eyes faded, to be replaced by the searing gleam of hunger. She couldn't sustain the heated stare and looked instead at her plate.

"Coward," he said.

She straightened her shoulders and lifted her chin. "I don't know what you mean."

"Yes, you do." He finished the meal and laid the fork down. He wiped his mouth and balled the napkin, then dropped it on the plate. "I'm through being easy with you."

The atmosphere sizzled between them.

He poured himself another cup of coffee, then paced from window to window, surveying every item in sight.

She opened her eyes wide as if in amazement. "Well, that's good to know. Does that mean you won't be grabbing me and kissing me when the mood strikes you the way you did at Amy's Christmas party? Or taking advantage of me when I'm injured and had a knock-out shot such as the night I broke my arm?"

He flung her one of those supremely male, all-knowing glances over his shoulder. "If you keep harping on those incidents, I'm going to think you miss my kisses."

"Huh."

"You liked 'em well enough. You responded...before you remembered you were trying to be the perfect widow to make up for the loss of the perfect husband—"

"You...you..." She was so furious she could hardly speak. "What do you know about it?"

"I know Clay wasn't perfect. He was a good cop and a good friend, but he wasn't perfect. He doesn't fit on that pedestal you're trying to force him on. That isn't love, Stephanie. That's obsession or guilt, maybe, but it isn't love."

"What do you know about love?" She stalked across the room.

Setting the mug aside, he turned and leaned his long, powerful body against the end of the counter. His eyes were like a mirror, gauging her actions without any emotion that she could detect. It made her furious.

"What do you know about missing someone so much you think you're going to die, but you can't because you have a child depending on you to keep his world on an even keel? What do you know about being responsible for that child growing into a man like his father, a man his father would be proud of?"

"It's a load of worry," he agreed. There was not an iota of sympathy in his manner. "Lots of people have done it. My father, for one. He had five kids to raise."

"He had a successful ranch and dairy...and a mother who moved in and helped with the kids."

"And just as much heartache as you, but he didn't become a martyr to it."

"Are you saying I have?" She wrapped her arms across her waist, holding her left one with her right.

His eyebrows rose slightly. His glance clearly conveyed an if-the-shoe-fits attitude. It wasn't the first time he'd accused her of hiding from reality.

"You don't understand—"

His hands closed on her shoulders and yanked her forward so that she was standing on her toes, her nose only inches from his.

"Understand what? How much it hurts to love someone and not have them? Tell me about it. How the longing can rise in you all sweet and hurting like sap in a cottonwood until you feel as if your heart is going to burst wide open? Tell me about it. How the emptiness gets to you when the moon comes up over a mountain, and you want to howl at it like some lonesome coyote lost from the pack? Tell me about it.''

Her blood ran as hot as his as she recalled nights in this house when she'd been that lonely, times when she'd thought she would die from it, times when she'd longed for *this* man to hold and comfort her.

"I know," she whispered fiercely. "God, yes, I know."

They were on shaky ground, teetering on the emotional precipice of disaster.

"Tell me about it, Steph," he continued in a hoarse voice as if she hadn't spoken. "And then let me tell you about other needs...like your own when we're together...or, heaven forbid, like mine."

"I know what your needs are, Nick. They're a thing of the moment. Passion isn't enough."

"Once," he said in the same low, hoarse tone, "I thought you were mine, that we'd be together, have a home, children—" He bit the rest of the words off as if realizing he'd said too much. "You said you loved me, but you went to another man."

She flinched from the accusation in his tone. For a second, she thought she saw agony in his eyes. She swallowed against the pain that filled her chest. "I did love you. I loved you with all the love a girl's heart could hold. You were my hero, my prince, my errant knight."

With trembling fingers, she reached up and smoothed the stubborn cowlick from his face, briefly lost in those long-ago days when they'd both been so young. She'd waited for his call, unable to believe he would abandon her like that.

"It was two years before I married. Two years, Nick. Think about that."

"You think I haven't?" he demanded. "You had a son with him, the man you married in my place."

"You mistook a moment of sadness for something more. You tried and judged me without giving me a chance to defend myself. Was that love? I don't think so. We shared a great passion, but love is more. It's trust and sympathy and caring."

"And Clay gave those to you?"

She hesitated, then nodded. She was no longer sure what she'd had with Clay. Their relationship had changed during the last years of their marriage. However, she'd been a faithful wife, never once letting herself think of Nick as anything but a friend after he'd returned to town.

He released her and walked out, his stride long and angry. He went to the stable and bent to study the ground. She saw him follow her footprints to the corner of the building, then he went inside to look around.

She stayed at the window until he came out and checked the tire prints in the dust where the cowboy had turned around. When he headed back toward the kitchen, she busied herself cleaning the skillet, not sure she could face him right now or that they should be alone in the house with emotion running so high between them—

A motor started up. She looked out the window in time to see Nick pull out of the drive, his expression as hard as stone.

Once he'd made her laugh with his endless teasing. He'd made her want to dance. Once he'd woven dreams for them out of moonbeams. Once they'd shared so much.

The need to cry that had overtaken her the previous night flooded her. She fought with it, refusing to be weak and give in as she had sitting out on the porch in the moonlight, the emptiness all around her. Oh yes, she could tell Nick a thing or two about loneliness.

She tried to figure out why they were quarreling about

the past after all this time. It was so senseless. There was the future to think of.

Nick, she realized, had never gotten over what he considered a bitter betrayal of their love.

She sighed as the sadness of it swept over her. She had to help him come to terms with their past so he could get on with his future. He would have to forgive her...and in doing so, himself, for not trusting their love.

Nick swore at himself all the way to town. To say those things, to hang his heart out on a string like a kite in the wind and expose himself like that... He cursed again.

A man had to keep things in perspective. Their youthful fling had been mostly hot blood and proximity. He'd sounded as if he still pined for her. He snorted in contempt for his stupidity. To say those things...

In town he stopped by the office and found the sheriff in. He gave the older man a rundown of the case.

The sheriff pulled at his lip. "What are you going to do?"

"Stake out the ranch and see if Greesley returns. He's looking for something. I may be wrong, but I'm betting it's the diamonds. I'll look around myself."

"I hope this doesn't look as bad as we think. It isn't only that the news will tarnish Clay's image, but the reputation of our whole force. He's looked upon as a hero."

"I know." And not only by the town folk. Stephanie had constructed an idealized version of her husband that no other man could ever match. She'd locked her heart away in a secret vault inside that ideal man. She'd never done that for him.

A girl's love, she'd called her feelings for him. Her words had seared his insides to cinders. His ears still burned with humiliation. Nothing like being a damn fool—

"So when are you going to move out to the ranch?"

Nick turned a baleful gaze on the sheriff.

"You'd better move in with Stephanie and her boy. I don't like them being out there alone."

"I mentioned it. She acted as if I'd suggested we do indecent acts in the town square." He frowned at the memory of what he'd actually said and cursed some more.

The sheriff chuckled. "Well, we can't let our citizens' sensibilities keep us from doing our job. We'll protect them whether they like it or not. You can tell her I said that."

"Yeah, I will." He returned the older man's sympathetic smile with an effort. He said goodbye and drove to his apartment. There he packed a few necessities, told his landlady he'd be in and out for the next few days and headed out of town.

At his ranch, he checked on the llamas and his own herd of registered beeves. After filling the stock tank with creek water, he opened a gate to let the cows graze in another meadow.

The lead cow was watching him, but she wouldn't be the first through the gate. A couple of her ladies-in-waiting would test the new area first. If they liked it, the queen would mosey in. When she did, the rest of the herd would follow.

Too bad people weren't as easy to handle.

With a frown he climbed into the truck and drove over to the fence between his property and the Double Bar S spread. He saw that they'd moved a herd into the field. He estimated a hundred cows plus their calves. There were a few yearlings left with the herd, those that hadn't sold last fall for some reason.

He checked the barbed wire fence and saw someone had made a few repairs to it within the past week. He scoped out the tire prints in the dirt at a bare spot. Almost bald. That cowboy had better get his mount reshod or he would be walking back to the bunkhouse one of these days.

The track wasn't the same as the one at Stephanie's place, so he didn't check it further. He returned to his truck.

A half an hour before dark, he eased off the highway onto the blacktop lane of the Bolt ranch. The name was depicted by a lightning bolt burned into a pine board and nailed to a post.

The pavement ended at the garage, a few feet from the lighted windows of the kitchen. Inside he could see Stephanie straightening up while Doogie sat at the table. The boy was talking, and they were both smiling.

A pain rippled in his chest as if his heart had undergone a brief spasm. He shook it off. He switched off the engine, climbed out and pocketed the key. He supposed he should announce his presence. He knocked on the door.

Stephanie's heart went into overdrive. She'd seen the truck drive up and park. Nick stood on the small porch off the kitchen, waiting to enter. Anger and sympathy fought within her. She willed them to go away. Common sense had returned. She didn't owe Nick a blasted thing.

"Who is it?" Doogie asked.

"Nick." She turned the dead bolt and opened the door. "Hi, what brings you out?" she asked brightly without inviting him in.

"Have you mentioned the Greesley character to Doogie?" he asked, without bothering with a greeting.

"Greesley?"

"The cowboy. He signed on with the Double Bar S. His story checks out. I guess he really was confused."

"Oh." Her heart rate slowed. She was relieved she wasn't going to have to argue with him about staying there.

"Hey, Nick, come on in. You want some cherry pie? Mom made one today. I'll get the plates."

Stephanie wished her son wasn't so generous at the moment. She was still reeling from their earlier encounter. She studied Nick with covert glances. He certainly didn't look any different from his normal self. His smile was as mocking as ever.

She pressed her lips together as emotions she couldn't begin to name flared in her. When he raised his eyebrows slightly, she realized he was waiting for her to second the invitation.

Nodding stiffly, she stepped back so he could enter and closed the door. As usual in the mountains, as soon as the sun went down, the air had cooled to frigid.

"You want ice cream?" Without waiting for an answer, Doogie got the carton out of the freezer and started dishing it on top of the pie wedges he'd placed on dessert plates.

"That would be nice." Nick went to the table.

Stephanie followed. "How long does the soccer season go on?" she asked, wondering how much longer she'd have to put up with Nick.

"Trying to get rid of me?" he asked with a wicked leer.

"Of course not." She shot a glance at Doogie. He was carrying two plates to the table, being careful not to drop the forks or let the ice cream drip over the side. He served the two adults, then went back for his own.

"This is great, isn't it?" Doogie said when he took his seat.

"It is. Thanks for the treat." Nick nodded his head to Doogie, then to her before taking a bite. "I need to stay here for a while," he announced.

"Hey, that's swell." Doogie radiated delight. "Isn't that great, Mom?"

She met Nick's gaze with an incredulous one. "You can't. It wouldn't look right."

"The sheriff wants me to keep an eye on things."

She couldn't think of an argument for that. She thought of the consequences of him being there, living with her and Doogie.

His words of anger rushed through her mind, and with them, the impression of anguish she'd so very briefly witnessed in his eyes. Those dark, dark, bitter chocolate eyes.

When Nick went out to look around the ranch, Doogie went with him. Stephanie pressed her forehead to the window, her heart acting up as she watched the two males stroll off into the dusk, their shoulders close but not quite touching, their voices rising and falling while they talked.

Guy talk, Clay used to call it. "You wouldn't understand," he used to tease her. "Important things, like what's the farthest you ever spit."

She wondered what Nick and Doogie were discussing with so much camaraderie. She listened to the sibilant hiss of her own sigh and tried to analyze the heaviness in her heart and its possible cause.

For some reason, their quarrel caused her to rethink her own life and realize how empty it had become. She'd used her work to block out the loneliness, so she wouldn't have to think about it.

She wondered if Nick did that, too.

He was thirty-four, and one of the county's most eligible bachelors. His little diatribe on loving and longing and being lonely had struck a chord in her. It was like listening to herself...if she'd had the courage to face her discontent.

She read for a while, then switched the TV on to catch the news. Doogie came in, said good-night and went to his room. The muscles in the back of her neck tensed as she waited for Nick to come in. When the news finished, she flicked off the set.

Going into the kitchen, she saw the truck was nowhere in sight. Good, Nick had had the good sense to leave.

She tried thinking of Clay, but his image wouldn't come, nor did the thought of the things they used to do together comfort her as it once had. Looking at the moonlight on the mountains, reflecting off patches of snow on the high peaks, she felt the longing Nick had spoken of, the feeling of being filled to the very brim with...something.

Fighting the ridiculous weepiness that had overtaken her lately, she fled to her room and went to bed, determined to put madness behind her, to live each day as it came and be a good mother to her son.

Chapter Seven

Stephanie snuggled under the covers and resisted getting up. Her sleep had been restless, filled with dreams depicting lots of meaningless activity. She'd awakened several times.

Monday morning she prodded herself with the reminder that she had to get up. Monday was the start of the six-day, ten-hour-a-day work week, plus the ranch chores and the house.

Mentally lashing herself, she jumped from the bed and rushed to the shower. The warm steam soothed the chill bumps. In twenty minutes she was dressed and ready to face the day.

The coffee was brewed when she entered the kitchen, thanks to the automatic timer. She poured a cup, needing the pick-me-up from the caffeine to counter the muzziness in her brain.

Glancing outside, she jerked in surprise as Nick came around the barn. Coffee splashed, hitting the counter, then her blue and beige cotton sweater and the beige slacks. "I'll boil him in oil," she declared, swabbing at the mess.

A moment later she heard his truck start and leave the house. She couldn't believe it. He'd startled her, then he'd driven off without a word.

Doogie came into the kitchen. "Was that Nick? I'd hoped he would have breakfast with us." Her son cast an accusing eye in her direction. "He slept in the truck because you were afraid people might talk. He stayed in the house when you hurt your arm, and nobody said anything."

"That was different." She swallowed a gulp of hot coffee.

The beast. The arrogant...unpredictable...*man*. He had spent the night. Without telling her.

However, knowing he was there, she might not have slept at all...or she might have slept better...if they had shared the night...and a bed.

Shocked at her wayward musing, she changed outfits and washed the stains out before they set. She told Doogie he could ride his bike to town. He'd been wanting to do that for ages, but she'd refused. She would let him try it a couple of times.

Driving to work shortly after that, she wondered if she was loosening up on her son because of Nick. Well, maybe. She'd see how it went. If Doogie couldn't handle the responsibility that went with greater freedom, she would ground him.

At the shop she arranged new merchandise and moved older items to the "bargain baskets" at each side of the door. They were a reliable source of income. Customers loved to browse through the baskets and find great buys.

At eleven the attorney who was going to update her will called and asked if she could join him for lunch.

She accepted. "Is one o'clock too late? Pat won't be in until then."

"That's great. I thought we'd go up to the resort."

She agreed, although that would take a bit longer than she'd had in mind. She had so much to do.

"This is lovely. The view always surprises me," she commented when the attorney pulled into the parking lot at The Summit resort. She could see the whole town, the lake where the community drew its water and the highway leading toward Denver.

The attorney's teeth flashed white against the attractive tan of his face. He was a tennis player and had already won the competition at the country club for males between thirty-five and fifty. She guessed his age to be thirty-eight from hints he'd given her about his life.

He'd married at thirty and was now divorced and the father of twin girls, aged seven, who lived with their mother. She wondered how he could bear to be apart from them. Clay had adored Doogie.

Nick liked children, too. He'd handled his niece with humor and firmness. He'd started the county youth program. He would make a wonderful father.

She pried her thoughts away from those lines.

Inside the resort she and the attorney were shown to a reserved table by the window. His light gray suit was a good foil for her dress of spring green with white trim. In her heels she was the same height as her escort, so that must make him six feet, a bit shorter than Nick.

As if she was having a dream, her thought seemed to conjure the deputy from thin air. When Stephanie glanced up, he was standing in the foyer of the restaurant, smiling pleasantly at the hostess, who was smiling right back. The woman led him to a table that also had a view, but was several over from hers.

Stephanie wondered who he was meeting.

"Wine?"

She smiled and nodded, then fixed her gaze firmly on the menu. "A Chablis," she requested. "The house brand."

By the time they'd ordered, Nick's party—the sheriff, his wife and a friend—had arrived. A female friend. People were always matchmaking for the county's most eligible bachelor.

She watched as Nick was introduced. He took the woman's hand in his and held it for a moment instead of giving it a shake. He seemed delighted to meet her. Fury danced like champagne bubbles in Stephanie's blood.

"Ahem." Her attorney was looking at her expectantly.

"I'm sorry. What did you say?"

"I was wondering why you hadn't moved to Denver. You seem much too cosmopolitan for the bucolic life." His tone was a verbal caress, his eyes appreciative.

His flattery was so practiced it was nearly a caricature of a compliment. "My home is here. My son and I like the area."

"Luckily for me."

No, she didn't think so. His flawless delivery and sincere expression were too smooth to be real. He peeled off admiring remarks the way her grandfather had been able to peel an apple in one long curly twist. To watch was entertaining, but the result was not the core of the matter, one might say.

She mentally grimaced at her pun. Hearing laughter, she turned her head and observed the foursome at Nick's table. His pleasant chuckle underscored the higher tones of his partner, who put her hand on his arm briefly as they shared some joke.

Stephanie tried to ignore the odd sensation that struck her in the chest. It was rather like having the breath knocked of her. She inhaled deeply until the sensation disappeared.

When their food was served, she kept her attention on it and didn't let her eyes drift down the room. She talked about her will and her worries about her son. "Clay's mom and my mother are too old to be saddled with a teenager. His youngest brother will take Doogie, but he doesn't want to handle the money. This trust fund sounds like the very thing."

"I'd advise three trustees. That's the usual number. Your attorney—" he smiled at her "—your banker and someone you trust who knows your son and will be willing to represent his best interests."

Her gaze strayed to Nick. He'd been Clay's friend. He was good with Doogie. And he'd do it out of duty if for no other reason. However, there was also Amy. "Yes, I have several people who would be willing. My partner for one—"

"She could have a conflict of interest concerning the shop," he warned.

That wouldn't be a problem for Nick. "Well, I'll think about it. You'll call me when you have everything ready? I'll decide on the trustees then."

"Of course." He signaled for the waiter. "They have delicious cheesecake here. Shall we have some?"

"No, thanks. I should get back."

Across the way, she saw Nick rise. He came toward them, his eyes taking in everything about her and her escort as he approached the table. A shiver of apprehension washed over her.

Nick could look very forbidding when he wanted, she'd discovered. In his uniform, with that gun strapped to his side, he was formidable. "Hello," she said when he came close.

He nodded to her, then to the other man.

The civilities between the men were casual, but she sensed undercurrents of male dislike. Jealousy? The thought sent a funny thrill along her nerves.

"I need to talk to you this afternoon," Nick said.

"I don't have any free time until five."

"I have some questions...official ones," he added when she opened her mouth to ask about them.

"Can you come by when the store closes, if that isn't too late?" she inquired politely.

"That's fine." He tipped a finger to his forehead. "I'll see you then. Oh, I'll be late getting in tonight. I need to stop by my place and pick up a pack of razors and some clothes. See you around, Counselor." He strode out of the restaurant.

Stephanie sat there, stunned by his announcement.

The attorney studied her with a disappointed slant on his handsome face. "So you and the deputy are close," he said.

"You could say that," she replied. Not as close as they were going to get when she saw him again. She was going to pull his black heart out by the roots and feed it to the crows.

Nick was madder than hell. The attorney was as smooth as his grandmother's caramel custard. The gleam in the guy's eyes when he'd looked at Stephanie was enough to set a man's teeth on edge. That was the second date for them.

Had the dude kissed her yet?

The thought had him gripping the steering wheel of the cruiser. When a driver ignored the solid yellow line and passed a long string of traffic, Nick hit the lights and pulled him over. By four that afternoon he'd given out thirty-three tickets, two mechanical-failure notices and a tongue-lashing to a load of teenagers who were crammed into a subcompact.

By the time he hit town, he had a headache. For another hour he went through the file boxes that detailed thirteen years of police work by Clay. He even found the résumé that Clay had submitted to the sheriff for a position here. His friend had been an outstanding cop in Los Angeles.

Clay's family had moved to this area when he'd been a kid, but he'd never talked much about them that Nick could recall. There were two older brothers, both in California, where his mom now lived. Strange how well you could know a person and yet not know him.

At the end of the hour, he hadn't found any leads or clues at all. He returned the files to storage and wandered through the office, where desks were jammed into every conceivable place and loaded with papers, reports in various stages of completion and even some zipped bags containing evidence.

He stopped at Clay's old desk. "Say, John, do you have any files left over from Clay? I need to check out a guy, and I think Clay might have had some information on him."

"All the reports went to storage, except for a couple of cases. One was that grand theft over at the cottage of that rich dude who comes up to fish. His cottage is bigger than my whole house." The deputy's smile was wry. "His daddy made their money in toilet paper. Go figure." He shook his head.

"Looks like I've hit a dead end." Nick pushed the

cowlick back and absently scratched his head. According to the sheriff, Clay hadn't been assigned to the robberies.

"How good are you at computers?" the older cop asked. "There're some files on the computer that I can't get into. I've never really needed to use them but the damned machine won't let me delete the directory until I clear out the files. I don't know the password."

"Passworded files? Yeah, I'll take a look if that's okay."

"Sure. I'll be out on the west section the rest of the week. Help yourself."

Nick glanced at his watch. It was time to go. He walked the short distance to the boutique. The Closed sign was on the door when he arrived. He went around back and knocked.

Stephanie let him in. She'd been waiting.

He was going to question her about Clay and the last months they'd spent together. A wife should know if a man had changed in any way the last few weeks of his life.

She wasn't going to like the interrogation.

Yeah, well, life was tough, and he had a job to do.

"Did you enjoy your lunch?" Stephanie asked with a fake smile. She stepped behind the desk, keeping it as a barrier between her and Nick while she thought of ways to do him in.

"Yeah, the food is always good at the resort."

"And the view. It's spectacular, isn't it?"

He looked her over while a slow smile bloomed on his sensuous mouth. "Yeah."

She resisted an urge to throw the stapler at his hard head. "If you ever lie about us again, I'm going to skin you alive and nail your hide to the barn door."

He laid a hand to his heart. "Me, lie? When did I lie?"

"At lunch today. You implied that you'd spent the night at the ranch—"

"I did."

She dropped the Miss Cordiality act and glared at him. "You made it sound as if you were a permanent fixture in my...in my..." She couldn't get the word past her lips.

"Bed?" he suggested, his dark eyebrows going up a notch. "Didn't you set him straight?"

She hesitated. "No."

"Why not?" He hooked his thumbs in his belt and watched her with colossal male arrogance.

"It was none of his business. Besides, I thought your surveillance was undercover."

"It is. Thanks for not blowing it, even at the risk to your own reputation." He paused. "That's the second time you've had lunch with him."

"It was business."

"Yeah, business." He was cynical.

She remembered the anguish in his eyes, as if she'd really hurt him all those years ago. For a second she wondered what might have been, how her life would have been different with this man. Unexpected pain darted through her heart. Maybe both of them needed to get over the past.

"What was this official duty you needed to see me about?"

He leaned against the door frame. "Clay. How would you describe his attitude the last few months before he died?"

After initial surprise at the topic, she considered the question. "What is that supposed to mean?"

"Did you notice a change in him, in his sleeping patterns or in his schedule?"

"No."

"Did he become irritable, silent, moody, withdrawn?"

"No." Her tone became sharper as she recalled those last few weeks.

"Did he suddenly have more money to throw around? Did he take you out to eat more often or go out by himself a lot? Did he buy things you or he had wanted but couldn't afford?"

She thought of the washer and dryer at the ranch. Clay had surprised her with them a month before his death. "No." Her denial was too quick.

Nick's gaze was filled with pity as well as irritation. "If I'm going to clear this up and put Doogie's mind to rest about his father, I have to know the truth, Stephanie. All of it."

"Clay bought a new washer and dryer," she said, angry with him for making her doubt her husband.

Nick shook his head. "He won the Superbowl pool down at the barbershop. He told us what he was going to do with the money."

She rubbed her arm, unable to look at Nick. The doubts about Clay came from herself, not him. "He was irritable, but that was because he'd stopped smoking. We quarreled—"

She stopped, but it was too late. Nick had already zeroed in on her confession.

"About what?"

"Nothing important."

"Let me decide that."

The silence throbbed like a bare, quivering heart laid open for observation. She swallowed. She cleared her throat. She swallowed again.

"Stephanie." It was a demand.

She shook her head and sighed. "It was about socks. I didn't get the washing done. He didn't have any clean socks to go with his uniform. I told him that he'd bought the washer and dryer, and he could damned well learn to use them if he wanted clean socks.''

She closed her eyes and saw her husband's face, the anger in his blue eyes, the hostility of his stare. She could feel her own frustration that he wouldn't understand her desire to have her own shop—

A hand touched her hair, smoothed it down and cupped her neck lightly. ''It's okay,'' Nick said on a husky note, his voice as strained as hers.

''I'll always regret that quarrel. It was so stupid. He left the house earlier than usual because of that. He died—''

''He died because of some loonie with a gun.''

''He left the house because of my temper—''

''He left because *he* was in a temper. Clay was responsible for his own actions.''

''I know, but that doesn't make the regret go away. Doogie was at the table. He looked so scared. It was the first time we'd ever quarreled in front of him, the first time we'd ever really yelled at each other.''

''Then Clay stomped out and died a hero,'' Nick said, his tone low and harsh. ''And you're determined to pay for that by being a martyr to his memory.''

''No.'' She shook her head. ''But it's hard. I felt guilty more than once for loving my work, for putting it before his wishes. I don't think I ever told him how much I cared.''

Nick held her gaze. ''He knew. There wasn't a day that went by that he didn't mention it in some way. He was proud of having a woman like you. You were the smartest, the sexiest, the best, and you were his. All the guys knew it. We envied him.'' He waited a beat, then spoke in his usual hard-edged manner to her. "We need to finish the questioning."

When he moved away from the desk, she took her chair. "What else do you need to know?"

"Lots. I want to search your place, not just the barn and stable, but the house, too. I want to go through Clay's clothing and personal items. I assume you still have them?"

"Some of them, yes. I gave his suits to charity."

He nodded. "All right. When would be a good time?"

She tried to think. "This weekend, I suppose. Did you see anything at the stable when you looked around there?"

"No. The weekend is too far away. I have tomorrow off. How about in the morning?"

"All right. I'll leave the door unlocked. You can go on in when you get there."

He studied her for a moment. "I'll be spending the night."

"That really isn't necessary. You said yourself that no one has been around."

"The ranch is too isolated for you and Doogie to be out there by yourselves. I'll hang around for a while."

She wasn't sure he should. "People will think that you…that we…"

"Cohabit?" he supplied coolly.

"Yes."

"No one can see me arrive or leave," he told her. "What does it matter what people think? You and I know the truth." He paused. "Are you afraid something will happen between us, or are you afraid that it won't?"

His mocking concern took her by surprise. "You wish," she snapped without thinking.

He gave a snort of laughter. "Yeah, I wish." His gaze

ran over her like molten chocolate, smooth, sweet and rich with forbidden delights, then he left.

Stephanie slowly forced each tense muscle to relax. Nick's insistence on staying at the ranch rattled her. She kept thinking of the possibilities.

She pushed her wedding band up and down her finger. The tears that had plagued her of late pressed against her eyelids. She was emotionally shaky these days. It was the oddest thing.

Nick arrived at the Bolt ranch later than he'd planned. The spitting llama had jumped the fence, the others had followed, except for a mother with a baby too young to jump that high. He'd spent two hours rounding them up.

That was strike two. He would have llama stew for sure next time that damned buck acted up.

Thunder rattled the windows of the truck when he parked behind the garage and out of sight of the outbuildings. The wind rocked the vehicle like a cradle. Good, maybe he'd sleep like a baby instead of lying awake and thinking things he shouldn't.

He tossed his pillow on the rumpled sleeping bag. He'd forgotten it last night, and his wadded jacket hadn't made a good substitute. Now if he had a warm, willing woman...

Ha.

He dashed to Stephanie's back porch and knocked. He'd let them know he was there in case something happened.

Doogie opened the door. "Are you staying here tonight?"

"Yeah. I'll be in the truck."

"Why don't you stay in the house? We're going to have a storm. There's a weather alert out."

Stephanie entered the kitchen, looking as sweet as a cherub. She wore a gown and robe. Her face was freshly scrubbed, her hair damp. The familiar tug of desire pulled at his common sense. He wanted to take her to bed—

"Mom, can't Nick stay in the house? Tell him about the storm. It could be dangerous."

Her mouth pruned up. "I'm sure he knows what's best."

Nick smiled wryly at the stilted answer. She probably hoped he'd get struck by lightning. "I'll be fine."

Doogie gave her an imploring glance, which she ignored. The boy gave a disgusted snort and returned to the table.

"Do you need anything?" she asked politely. "You're welcome to use the shower."

"No, I just came from my place. I'll see you in the morning. I wanted to remind you to leave the door unlocked when you left for work so I can get in."

Doogie jumped on his statement and demanded to know what was going on.

"Deputy Dorelli wants to look through your father's things for a clue to the stranger you saw watching me," Stephanie explained.

"So you are investigating him." Doogie's eyes gleamed with excitement.

Nick nodded. "He was on the force in L.A. with your dad. The records show he got into trouble down there. The sheriff and I wonder what he's doing up here."

"I'll help you catch him. What do you think he's done?"

"Not a thing. We might be wrong in our thinking." Nick tipped his hat to mother and son. "Good night. I'll see you in the morning."

* * *

Stephanie locked the door securely after Nick disappeared into the dark. She shooed Doogie to bed and turned off the light as they walked down the hall.

"We should have invited Nick to sleep inside," Doogie said, standing in his doorway. "I think it's pretty crummy to make him sleep in his truck."

"We didn't make him do anything. It's totally unnecessary for him to be here."

"But that guy was nosing around."

"You heard Nick…the man's story checks out. There's nothing for us to worry about. Good night," she said firmly.

Her son closed his door with enough force to indicate his feelings, but not enough to make her have to reprimand him. Shaking her head, she went to her room and climbed into bed. She actually went to sleep rather quickly.

Three hours later she awoke with a start. The rain beat against the house as if demons were knocking on it with clubs. She realized the rain had turned to hailstones, and she worried about the windows. It sounded hard enough to crack glass.

She thought of Nick, outside in his truck.

Burrowing deeper into the pillow, she tried to shut out the image. The house swayed and creaked as the storm slammed into it, driving waves of rain, sleet and hail before it in its fury.

Cold air caressed her face. The temperature had dropped close to freezing as it often did when a storm roared down from the mountain peaks, no matter what time of year it was.

She wondered if Nick was warm enough.

Her conscience wouldn't let her drop back into sleep. She fought it for twenty minutes. Then, with a groan, she flung the warm covers back and yanked on her loafers and a robe. At the back door she grabbed a poncho and an umbrella. She found the garage door remote control in her purse, pressed the button and headed outside.

The wind almost jerked the umbrella out of her hand when she stepped onto the porch. She clutched it tighter and ran across the sodden grass. In the brilliant flashes of lightning, she saw the truck parked beside the garage. She knocked on the window.

He opened the door. "What the hell?" Nick exclaimed. He grabbed her arm and dragged her up and into the seat. He slammed the door. After closing the umbrella, he tossed it on the floor along with the poncho she'd brought for him.

"What are you doing out in this?" he demanded. "Have you lost your mind?"

"Yes." She was shivering. "Drive into the garage. The hail will ruin your truck."

He slid away from her and cranked up the truck. After backing up and angling into the right position, he pulled forward into the vacant space in the garage where Clay's cruiser used to be. The sounds of the storm receded somewhat. He turned the engine off. "Now you want to tell me what the hell you're doing out here?"

"It's cold. You should come into the house." She wrapped her arms across her middle. Shivers coursed through her.

He heaved a sigh. "Why didn't you call the dispatcher and have him call me on the radio?"

"I didn't think of it." She wished she hadn't come. She felt cold and miserable.

"You're freezing, you little fool."

It seemed ungrateful of him to criticize her when she'd risked life and limb to come out in the rain. She sniffed.

"Ah, hell," he muttered. His voice was husky. He pulled her across the bench-type seat and tucked her in close beside him. He rubbed her arms until she was warm again.

The porch light cast dancing shadows into the garage through the veils of rain. She felt his lips touch her hair, then her temple. She bit her bottom lip to stop a sigh from escaping. His warmth was all around her, soothing and exciting.

The storm descended again, lashing through the open garage door as if trying to reach them. She thought of the rain. She thought of drowning in the passion they'd once shared.

He'd been her first love, this man who was no longer a boy, but a stranger who excited her as much as her youthful lover. He also disturbed her with his cynical harshness.

He laid his hand on her waist and brought her closer. He rubbed along her side. He reached her breast and paused. She thought of the storm. She thought of the wisdom of coming out in it to tell him to sleep in the house.

When he at last kissed her, she stopped thinking at all.

He varied the pressure from soft to hard to soft. He angled his head one way, then the other. When his tongue stroked across her lips, she opened to him. The pounding of the blood through her body obliterated the sounds of the storm.

She turned toward him and wrapped her arms around his shoulders. His flannel shirt was warm from his body. She found the hem and slipped her hands inside. His skin was smooth. The muscles flexed as he moved so they were touching along their chests and thighs.

When he slipped one arm under her knees and lifted, she held on while he slid over, then set her in his lap. She could feel the thud of his heart against her. Her own kicked an irregular beat on her rib cage. His body was hard, ready to claim her.

The wind swirled into the garage and gently rocked them. The storm outside was no more turbulent than the one raging inside her. She clung to him, shaken by a tempest of emotions she couldn't identify.

She tilted her head back on his arm while he ravished her neck with sweet, sweet kisses.

Her mind was hazy with the madness he induced. Her body glowed with an inner fire. She caressed through his thick hair, loving the springy stubbornness of his cowlick. His hands, so gentle in their caresses, moved over her. She wanted him more than she'd ever wanted or needed him before.

The never-forgotten familiarity of his touch was comforting as well as exciting. She realized she'd never completely let it go, this first sweet love of hers.

"Oh, love," she whispered, crushed by this need for him. It overpowered anything she'd ever felt in the past for anyone, including him.

Nick pulled away with a curse. He caught her hands and held them. His voice, when he spoke, was as raw as the storm, and just as furious. "Damn you," he said. "Damn you for making me want you, for making me forget—" He broke off. "We'd better go inside before the storm gets worse."

For a moment she couldn't move. Common sense returned with a rush of humiliation and confusion. "Yes, but first we need to talk."

"About what?"

She laid a hand on his arm. "I've been thinking about us for days now."

"Yeah, you and me both."

"Sometimes it seems as if we're in a time warp, that we've returned to the past. It's almost as if we're trapped in the emotions of that time. For both our sakes, I think we need to talk this out and then maybe we can get on with our lives."

"My life is fine."

He sounded the very essence of the affronted male. She would have smiled if the situation weren't so perilous. "Why didn't you marry the woman you were engaged to?"

"We weren't compatible."

"Oh."

"Did that shoot holes in your theory of the unresolved past?" He leaned over her, his face lit momentarily by a flash of lightning. Its shape remained on her retina long after the light was gone.

"No. I think it's true. We never quite got over each other. We never forgave each other for wrongs, whether real or imagined. I think we need to come to grips with that."

"I think we've talked enough." His mouth descended on hers again, hard this time, as if to shut her up.

She let the kiss go on, not encouraging him, but not pushing him away, either. She couldn't. This was Nick, her first love. She had to help him overcome their past. As for the future, she couldn't think that far ahead right now. She clutched his arms and resisted the wild hunger.

He lifted his mouth away and sighed heavily. "Let's go in, Steph. Much more of this and I won't let you out of the truck until morning. Then we'll both have regrets."

Chapter Eight

Nick woke in the guest bed the next morning. His thoughts flew to the night. Stephanie had faced the storm to tell him to come inside. He had, but first he'd held her and kissed her.

For wild, endless minutes the storm outside had held them prisoner while the one inside had consumed them. In those moments he'd have given his soul for her.... No, no more. He'd learned that lesson long ago.

Forget the past, he ordered. Much more important to this time and place was the passionate interlude in the storm. He needed to think about it rationally. He rubbed a hand over his eyes, too weary to think at all.

Both he and Steph had been shaking when they'd climbed out of the truck and made a dash for the house. It wasn't until they were on the porch that either of them remembered the umbrella and poncho. She'd apologized without looking at him.

He thought of making love to her in the truck. In the back with the down sleeping bag to soften their bed and passion to keep them warm. It was something he'd wanted to do with her for a long time. A fool's dream. He wasn't a boy any longer, holding tight to fantasies that existed only in his own mind.

If he were smart, he'd put his application in for the Denver police force and move down there. Maybe he would. As soon as he solved this case.

Looking at the window, he saw the sky was dark and sullen. The clock indicated he'd slept until nine. With an exclamation, he leapt from bed and headed for the shower.

In the kitchen he found a pot of coffee brewed. A note beside the coffeemaker told him to help himself to the rolls and coffee and that the boxes containing Clay's things were in the guest bedroom closet.

A plastic container of fresh pastries was on the counter. He chose a cherry-filled one and strolled into the study with it and a mug of coffee in hand, his mind focused on his job.

A computer of vintage age was nestled into a wall unit. He turned it on and checked out the directory. He found Doogie's homework and the family telephone numbers and addresses, but nothing of interest to his investigation. He'd spent a few minutes of the previous day on Clay's files at the office, but hadn't been able to crack the password to the directory. He hoped to turn up a clue here at the ranch.

Summoning the patience he'd learned in his years of police work, he went through each file on the computer. In addition to homework, he found games and educational programs for Doogie. He skimmed through Stephanie's personal finances and her business plans for the shop. She was practical as well as smart.

Four hours later he was satisfied that he hadn't missed anything important. He would run a disk check for deleted files and repair the fragmented ones so Steph's programs would run faster, but right now, he was hungry.

Standing, he stretched and went into the kitchen for a drink of water. He'd finished off the coffee long ago. Grimacing at the sweet rolls, he decided to turn off the computer and go to town for lunch. He headed down the hall, then remembered he hadn't checked Clay's personal items. He'd do that first.

In the guest room he found the boxes as promised, all lined up on the closet floor. He opened the first one and found Clay's old uniforms. He went through the pockets of each piece, then went to the next box. The last box was personal items—notes, letters and, to his surprise, a set of journals.

Feeling like an interloper, he opened a journal and began reading. He soon caught on to Clay's shorthand. A lot of it was standard police code. The journals were a complete set of cases that Clay had worked on, going back to his rookie year. It looked as if Clay had been planning to write a book when he retired, maybe become another bestselling author of police procedural novels.

Putting the journals in order, he found the final one and began to read the entries for the last year of Clay's life. There were references to "S" and "D," easily interpreted as Stephanie and Doogie, notes about picking up his son from school, about Stephanie being late getting home, then finally pay dirt—a mention of the robberies at the resort and summerhouses, including the diamond necklace, worth a cool three hundred thousand, that had been stolen.

That was the last note, dated two days before his death.

Nick replaced the journals in the closet. He walked down the hall and paused outside the master bedroom.

Longing hit him like a sneak blow to the body, low and

unexpected. His muscles tensed and cramped with the need to have her. Last night he nearly had. Until she'd whispered the words she'd once spoken to him exclusively, and he'd remembered they were a lie. She hadn't been his love.

He ran a hand over his forehead where a headache pounded dully. Against all common sense, he entered the room. He breathed in slowly, taking in the subtle scent of Stephanie that pervaded the air. He remembered where he'd found her nightgown, handily tucked under her pillow.

It was one of those intimate revelations that stayed with a man. Heat gathered low in his body.

She'd shared this room with another. Her husband. For the first time he thought about why she and Clay had waited two years to marry. She'd graduated from the community college, then worked a year at the local bank before taking the plunge. She'd intimated she'd been waiting for him to come back.

He'd been waiting for her to contact him, full of remorse. He'd already planned his speech of forgiveness. He realized how sanctimonious that sounded. He'd been so sure he was right and she was the one in the wrong. He clenched and unclenched his fists as old pain assailed him.

He'd thought of going to her, but as the weeks dragged by, it had become harder. When he'd returned home for the summer, he'd seen Steph coming out of the coffee shop with Clay. She'd looked at him and the girl he was with, then had looked away as if she didn't know him.

That had hurt. Maybe Steph was right. Maybe they did need to forgive each other and get on with their lives.

The sounds of a car engine broke into his musing. From the kitchen window, he saw Stephanie arrive home. She parked in the garage and lifted a bag out of the back of the car before heading for the house. He glanced at his watch.

One o'clock. Tuesday was her half day, he remembered. He went to meet her. "Let me help." He took the bag from her and carried it inside. "Anything else?"

Stephanie shook her head. She hadn't thought Nick would still be there. "Aren't you through yet?"

"Pretty much. I went through the last box a few minutes ago and found Clay's journals. Did you know he kept them?"

"Yes. The sheriff read through them two years ago. He didn't find anything suspicious." She sounded defensive but couldn't help it. She couldn't look at Nick.

Going to his truck last night had been foolish. Letting him kiss her had been irresponsible. Trying to talk to him had been futile. He wasn't going to listen to anything she said.

"Clay seemed to be working with some undercover cop. He mentioned the rash of robberies we had at the ski resort and the one at the summerhouse. His notes indicated he had an inside informer."

She nodded. "Someone he called 'B.' I don't know who it was," she added, to waylay the question she could see forming in Nick's eyes.

"Bob Greesley, alias Greenwood, comes to mind."

"Yes."

"Why didn't you tell me about the journals?"

"I haven't thought of them in months. I've had other things on my mind. The sheriff knew about them."

She didn't have time for the turbulent emotions of her youth or for the wild passion Nick stirred in her. She was a woman now, one with responsibilities. She and Nick couldn't ever go back to being young and madly in love again.

"He probably forgot. I guess you did, too." His anger with her was almost palpable.

"Yes." She looked him in the eye. "I did."

"It doesn't matter. The journals weren't much help. Did Clay have any passwords he used for his computer files?"

She did remember that. "His mother's name."

Nick looked disappointed. "I tried her maiden name."

Stephanie shook her head. "It was her middle name. Cornelia after her grandfather. She said a cousin she hated called her Corny all the time after he'd found out and she'd never used it again. After she married, she used the initial of her maiden name rather than her middle name."

"Well, that gives me something to go on. I'd like to go over the journals with you." He hesitated, then studied her. "Can you handle it?"

She slipped her shoes off and started putting the groceries away. A strand of hair slipped over her cheek when she shook her head. She hooked it behind her ear. "It hurt when I read them the first time," she admitted. "I hadn't realized I was late so much." She sighed. "Why is it okay for a man to be immersed in his job but not the woman?"

"Because someone has to tend the home fires. It's usually the woman. Men expect it, even if the woman also works outside the home."

"It isn't fair."

"No, but that's the way it is." He straddled a chair. "Or the way it used to be. Times are changing."

She couldn't help but note the way his casual clothing fit his tall, lean body. She folded the paper bag and put it under the sink. She remembered how hard his muscles were, how warm his body was, how *good* it had felt to slide her hands over him.

"I need to go by the office, then I'll stop for lunch. Is it okay if I come back later and go over the details with you, say, in a couple of hours?" His tone was formal.

"Yes." She hesitated. She'd planned on having a sandwich since Doogie was staying in town with a couple of friends. "I...we could have sandwiches if you'd like. That way we could get through the journals this afternoon."

"What about Doogie?"

"He's gone to a movie."

He considered, then nodded. "Sandwiches will be fine."

After he left, she went to the bedroom to change into a pair of shorts and a top. She was shaky inside. So they'd be alone all afternoon. It didn't mean anything. Unless she wanted it to. Her heart fluttered at the thought. Sweet, painful hunger rushed over her. She wanted him, but did she want more?

She straightened the house, washed sheets and remade the beds. When Nick returned, he brought the last of Clay's journals with him. They went into the study. He read a page from it. She stopped by his chair and read over his shoulder.

"S" late again today. Can't wait for her. She gets mad when I'm not home. I get mad when she doesn't come in on time. We're at a standoff. Home life like work, getting nowhere.

The anger and accusation in the last statement hurt. Nick looked up at her. "Sounds as if marriage can be tough. It's probably better that I've never tried it." His snort of laughter was edged with irony, but she heard more now—

longing, perhaps, and loneliness, and dreams that had never quite died no matter how cynical he tried to be.

She realized she was beginning to know Nick in a different way than in their senior year of high school and their first year of college. They'd each had so much to learn about life....

"It can be wonderful, too." She suddenly wished he'd found someone and been happy. It upset her that he hadn't. He deserved more from life.

She pushed her ring up and down on her finger. It flew out of her hand and disappeared under the sofa.

"I'll get it." He bent and searched until he found it. He lifted her hand and slipped it back into place. "Getting loose," he mentioned. "Are you losing weight?"

"No, it's always been a little big."

She looked at her hand in his, his long slender fingers moving the ring around and around.

"When are you going to stop wearing it?" he asked on a different note.

"I don't know. Soon, maybe."

Releasing her, he gave a grunt as if it had been an idle question and he really didn't care. His seemingly careless attitude caused an ache in her chest. She was tempted to brush the cowlick off his forehead and press him to her breast, the way she would comfort her son. It was probably insane of her to think this strong, arrogant male needed her sympathy.

She flexed her injured hand. "Nick, about last night." A need to talk about them and where they might be going overcame her. She felt they were on the verge of discovering something new in their relationship.

"Last night was a mistake."

The quick, flat statement stopped her in her tracks. It

was a total denial that anything important had happened between them.

After one intense, angry glare, he walked out, leaving her standing there with her pity in her hand. Feelings she'd forgotten for years welled up in her.

She'd often been uneasy during the past year when she was around Nick. She realized what it was. She was in danger of falling in love with him again, not with a girl's love for the boy he had been, but with a woman's love, deep and rich and abiding, for the man he had become.

Her legs trembled so that she had to sit down. She held her hands against her heart in order to contain it.

"Oh, Nick," she murmured. "What fools we've been."

She lifted her hand. Slowly she removed the ring. She'd loved her husband. He'd filled so many empty places in her life. He'd brought her laughter and love when she'd needed them so desperately. Her love for Clay had been based on respect and friendship as much as passion.

Her love for Nick had been driven by youthful passion and starry-eyed expectations that were about as realistic as wishing on a star. The odd flash of agony in his eyes when they'd quarreled came back to her.

They'd hurt each other all those years ago. She'd waited for him to apologize. He'd waited for her to explain. They'd both been too full of pride to go to the other.

The past few months had been filled with strain. The struggle between them, the anger, the passion, did those things mean they were falling in love all over again?

Maybe. It was something to think about.

Stephanie flexed her hand experimentally. "My arm feels so light."

The doctor chuckled. "Well, it did lose some muscle

while you had the cast on. Take it easy for another couple of weeks. You can remove the support after you finish your chores.''

The cast had been replaced by a device with a metal piece to support her wrist. It was covered with cloth that encased her arm and closed with Velcro fasteners.

Returning to the store, she worked until a few minutes before three. ''See you tomorrow,'' she said to Pat, who was going to close up while she went to the final soccer game of the season. Doogie's team was playing the number-one team, for the county championship.

The bleachers were crowded when she arrived. She searched the sea of faces for a place.

''Mom, down here.''

She turned toward her son's voice. He was beckoning her down to the row of seats behind the Bear Tooths' bench. He'd saved a place for her. She made her way to it and held up her hand.

Doogie gave her a high five, then bounded back to the bench to gather the last words of wisdom from their coach.

''Good luck,'' she called.

Nick's head swung around. His eyes met hers. He smiled and nodded, a perfunctory greeting the same as he gave other parents.

With a start she realized she missed the way he used to greet her—with his eyes alight, his smile slow and appreciative. He'd made her feel special.

But that had been so many years ago. She missed him, that young man who had filled her heart to overflowing.

Vanity. Everyone liked to be admired and thought well of. Nick didn't think well of her at all. He thought she'd betrayed their love. He'd avoided her since they'd gone through Clay's journals earlier that week.

She touched her lips, recalling the warm feel of his mouth on hers. Her mental processes became muddled when she recalled sitting in his lap and returning kiss for kiss. It no longer embarrassed her. She'd wanted him to make love to her, but he'd pulled back. She wondered why, if he wanted her the way his eyes sometimes said he did—

"Okay, team, let's show 'em what we can do." Nick's rich baritone penetrated her thoughts.

She clapped with the rest of the fans when the teams took their places. The game was fast. The other team was larger than the Bear Tooths, but they weren't as fast. Doogie and his teammate Ty seemed to be everywhere on the field. They yelled encouragement and directed the ball handler to an open player. The two boys were the leaders. Pride filled her.

When the Tooths scored, Stephanie was on her feet, cheering as loudly as any proud parent. When she sat down, she caught Nick's glance. On an impulse, she gave him a "V for victory" sign.

He gave her a half smile, then resumed his duties as head coach of the underdogs. His eyes held a brooding quality, as if he, too, had been doing a lot of thinking.

At halftime, the score was tied at one all. The last quarter, it was tied at two all. Things hadn't changed by the bell. The game went into overtime. The noise level in the stands climbed by several decibels. Someone started a wave, and they all stood and raised their arms as excitement swept over the crowd. Stephanie had never felt so alive.

She wondered how the players could hear the coaches' instructions as they prepared for the final attempt at the county championship.

The play-off began. The crowd settled down like

schoolkids when the teacher walked into the room. It didn't last long.

The Hogs made a goal. Their side of the bleachers went wild. Stephanie shouted encouragement to the Tooths. They made a goal. She shrieked like a banshee. Again Nick glanced her way. She winked at him.

He shook his head and went back to work.

The last two minutes passed in a blur. The ball changed sides several times. Then Doogie had the ball. He raced up the field. Ty broke loose from the pack and ran after him.

The Hogs' goalie was ready, his eyes on Doogie and the ball. At the last second Doogie kicked the ball hard to the left. Ty kicked it in.

"We won," Stephanie screamed. She winced as a pain shot up her left arm. Glancing down, she realized she'd been clapping so hard her hands were fiery red. Her arm ached. She rubbed her wrist and joined in the cheer. "Yea Tooths!"

"Pizza for everyone," she heard Nick shout to his players.

An hour later Stephanie came face-to-face with him at the pizza place in town. The room was a riot of activity as the players recalled their moments of doubts and glory.

"Dorelli can pull a win out of a hat every time," one of the opposing coaches grumbled in admiration and envy.

Stephanie couldn't suppress a surge of pride. Doogie had been voted the most valuable player. Even she recognized it had taken an extra ounce of maturity to pass the ball off, thus catching the goalie off guard, so that Ty could make the winning score. She spoke to other parents and congratulated the players. Biting the bullet, so to speak, she stepped forward.

Nick stood with one of the men who acted as assistant

coach. She spoke to both of them, then forced herself to look at Nick. "You must be feeling very proud," she began.

"I'm proud of the team." His expression was unreadable. It was like talking to a wall of granite. He'd closed himself off from her, his softer feelings locked in some impenetrable place.

There was nothing she could say to him in a crowd, anyway. "Yes. Well, I'd better tell Doogie I'm leaving. I agreed to do his chores if the Tooths won."

"Is he staying in town with the rest of the gang?"

"Yes. Ty's father has invited the team to his house for a celebration sleepover."

"Hmm." He checked his watch. "I need to head out to my place to check on the livestock, too."

It was clearly a dismissal. She said good-night and went to find her son. After speaking to him, she drove out of town. There was an unusual number of cars on Main Street. The result of the championship game. Everyone was eating out.

The road to the ranch was deserted. She pulled into the drive, her spirits dragging a bit. She didn't know how to tell Nick what was wrong between them. His distant attitude was no help at all in resolving the situation.

She'd missed him this week. He'd decided he was mistaken in the intentions of the ex-cop from L.A. The man was highly competent, and the owner of the Double Bar S was pleased with his work, according to Nick. The surveillance had been dropped.

Life was back to normal. School would start on Monday, so Doogie would be busy with that. Eighth grade. Her son was growing up. Five years and he would be off to college. He'd have friends she didn't know, a whole life without her.

Don't get maudlin, she scolded when her throat clogged with emotion. Honestly. She pulled into the garage and parked.

Going into the house, she set her purse on the counter and stood there for a minute. The silence breathed on her like a sultry sigh. She left the back door open to let the air circulate and drive out the August heat.

She started to kick her shoes off, then decided to go to the bedroom before she shed her town clothes. Entering the bedroom, she halted as a twinkle caught her eye. She took two steps forward. The hair on her neck prickled.

A penny. What was a penny doing in the middle of her bedroom carpet?

She glanced toward the closet. The door was closed. She usually left it ajar.

The urge to flee nearly gave her away. She controlled it. "Darn," she said aloud, annoyed. "I forgot the milk."

She scurried out of the bedroom. In the kitchen, she snatched her purse as she went out the door. She didn't look back. In the car, she locked the doors, then pushed the key in the ignition, her hand visibly shaking. She backed out carefully, even paused to adjust the air-conditioning in case he was watching from the bedroom window, then headed out.

She swept the stable area with a quick perusal on her way down the drive. There was no sign of the black pickup. By the time she drove down the county road a half mile and turned off on the gravel drive to Nick's place, her heart had slowed. She was beginning to feel foolish. She looked for a place to turn around.

A cruiser rounded the curve behind her and slowed when the driver saw her. Nick stayed on her tail until she reached the open space in front of his cabin. She rolled down the window.

He climbed out of his vehicle and strode over. "Miss your driveway?" he inquired. He watched her with wary curiosity.

"No. I...I thought someone was at the house." She made a deprecating gesture. "I panicked and ran."

"Did you see anyone?"

"No. It was foolish." She wished she could disappear in a cloud of dust. "I saw a penny on the carpet in my bedroom. I must have dropped it last night."

"You don't leave things lying on the floor. Anything else?"

"Not really. The closet door was closed. You have to push it hard to get it to latch. I rarely do." She glanced at him, expecting to see exasperation.

He looked thoughtful. "I'll go over and check it out. You can wait here."

"Oh, no. That's all right. Really, it's nothing. Just a case of nerves."

"I'll decide that." His manner was curt. His direct gaze made it clear he was a cop and he was in control. Then he reached in and removed her keys. He jammed them in his pocket and headed for the cruiser.

"Wait a minute," she called after him. "You can't leave me stranded out here." She jumped out and ran after him. She caught him at the cruiser and put a hand on his arm to stop his climbing in and taking off.

"Stay out of this," he warned. "I'll let you know when you can return to your place."

She dropped her hand. His glance took in the wrist support and the fact that the cast was gone. He dug the keys out of his jeans and dropped them in her palm.

"Stay here until I come back."

"No. It's my house. I know my rights."

"Get in my way and I swear I'll shoot you." His sharp retort smarted.

"I know to stay out of the way. I wasn't a cop's wife for all those years for nothing."

"Yeah," he said. He jumped into the cruiser and was gone.

His harsh reminder to stay out of the way lingered in her mind as she followed several yards behind the cruiser.

If anyone had been at her place, he'd have left by now if he had any sense. Unless he was a madman. A chill chased up her arms. Or an ex-cop who was trained to kill.

Nick was already in the house when she stopped beside his truck. She climbed out but stayed by her car. If anything happened, she wanted to be near, but she knew not to go barging in. She tried not to think of anyone getting hurt.

"Okay," Nick called from the door.

She joined him in the kitchen. "Did you find anything?"

"Nothing. Not even a penny."

"Nothing?" She hurried to the bedroom. The closet door was open, the penny was gone. The hair stood up on her nape. "It was right there," she insisted, pointing to the spot. She faced Nick. "It twinkled in the light."

"I believe you." Nick indicated the closet. "He left a set of footprints in there in the carpet. Looks as if he was wearing standard issue cowboy boots. The size is too big to be yours. I assume Doogie doesn't hang around in your closet."

"Of course not." She peered into the closet. "What do you think he wanted?"

Nick shrugged. "Money. Jewelry. The missing necklace if it was our cowboy." The fury simmered in him. If he'd found the guy in her bedroom, he probably would have shot him. He tamped the anger down. He was there strictly as a cop. He wasn't the outraged husband whose domain had been invaded.

She went to her dresser and opened the jewelry box. It played the theme from *Beauty and the Beast.* "Why didn't he look in my jewelry case? It has a few good pieces—my grandmother's opals, some cultured pearls."

He walked over and studied the contents. "Nothing missing?"

"No." She opened a shallow drawer under the main section. The few pins and a gold bracelet gleamed against the burgundy velvet. "It's all there."

"No secret compartments?"

"Not that I know of."

He picked up the case and studied the back. No signs of a hidden drawer or false bottom. An idea formed in his mind, one that had niggled at the back of his consciousness since he'd cracked Clay's closed files with the password Steph had given him. "I think I know what happened to the necklace."

Chapter Nine

"What?" Stephanie couldn't prevent the quiver in her voice at Nick's ominous statement.

"Clay was on to something. I checked the computer files at the office. The password you gave me worked."

"I'm glad." She was. She would face the truth no matter how much it might hurt and no matter how much Nick might try to protect her from that truth. "What did the files contain?"

"Details of the burglaries Greesley had committed in L.A. and a comparison of the ones in this area. Clay was suspicious of Greesley's motives for being in town, especially after the thefts started. He was keeping an eye on him."

"But what about the conversation Doogie overheard? Greesley wanted to know what Clay did with the diamonds. Wouldn't that indicate Clay was in on the deal?"

"No. When Greesley accused Clay of having them, Clay realized what I just figured out. Greesley didn't commit the burglary at the summer house, although he probably was responsible for the ones at the resort.''

"I don't understand."

"I think the other burglaries were to cover the main one, the theft of the diamonds. Clay realized that, too. Greesley was supposed to steal the necklace, but someone beat him to it."

"Who?"

"That's what I'm going to figure out. I want to check through your computer here one more time."

A weight rolled off Stephanie's soul. She realized she had doubted Clay since she'd learned of the conversation Doogie had overheard. She followed Nick into the home office.

"I want to work with you on this," she said, following him down the hall.

"There's no need." He paused. "I could be wrong. You might end up getting hurt."

"I'd rather face the truth, Nick, whatever it is. You would have to tell me eventually, at any rate. You're too honest to hide something this important in our lives."

He stopped by the computer. "You think I'm honest?"

She nodded.

"Huh."

"But stubborn," she added.

Without another word, he turned on the computer, leaving her standing in the middle of the floor, her mouth crimped in wry amusement while he frowned in obvious irritation.

Nick pulled a second chair up beside the desk and took a seat in front of the computer. Stephanie sat beside him, their shoulders almost touching. Nick began a systematic search. In a separate partition, he found a hidden directory.

"I hope he only used one password," Nick muttered when he called up a file.

The computer printed a series of meaningless symbols on the screen, then returned so that the password would be printed over the symbols and not be readable to anyone who watched. Nick typed in Cornelia.

The file closed.

"Damn, that worked at the office," he said. He called up the second file. Same thing. "No luck. I don't know what else he might have used."

"Corny," Steph suggested.

Nick gave her a skeptical glance, but tried again. This time the computer took the word, opened the file, then gave a list of three options. Nick chose the one labeled "GL," for grand larceny, he assumed.

Again they hit a passworded section.

He tried the same word. The computer closed the file. Nick opened it again and went back to the same list.

"Any other suggestions?"

Stephanie ran through the possibilities. "Well, Cornelia was his mother's middle name and Corny the nickname she hated. Douglas is Doogie's middle name and Doogie the name he prefers—"

Nick was already typing *Doogie* before she finished. "Bingo," he said with a low laugh.

The murmur of that sound zeroed in to a secret spot inside her and started it pulsing. Later, she promised her heart. When the case was resolved. Then it would be time for them.

"My God," Nick said.

She leaned over his shoulder. The evidence was laid out before them. Clay had caught on to the series of robberies. The perpetrator had been the ex-L.A. cop. But at the instigation of the owner of the necklace.

"The other burglaries were to cover the theft of the necklace," Nick explained. "Steph, Clay didn't leave the house early because of a quarrel with you." He pointed to a line on the screen. "He had a meeting with Greesley that morning. At the quick market."

His eyes, when he turned to her, were filled with pity.

She drew a steadying breath. "It's all right. I can handle it," she said. The implications that Nick with his trained investigative mind had already understood became clear to her.

"Clay was going to arrest his old friend. He had the last bit of evidence. Look at the bank account he discovered," Nick continued. "The amount of money in it is large, a payoff to Greesley for the robberies."

"The one at the market was a setup," she said.

Nick stared at the screen for a second without saying anything. "Yes."

"Greesley killed Clay and made it look like robbery. Then he left town until things cooled off. He came back to find the necklace."

"Yes."

"Such a waste," she whispered. "Such greed. Why?"

"Clay figured it out. The son of the toilet paper magnate from Denver needed money. He wasn't the businessman his father had been. Clay documented the guy's spending habits and debts. Also the insurance payoff, which kept the son from having to declare bankruptcy. It's all here, enough to convict both of them. I'm going to call the sheriff. I think he'll want to know about this right away."

"But what happened to the necklace?"

"I think we'll ask the son that question." Before picking up the phone, he clasped her shoulders. "I'm sorry, Steph. There'll be a lot of publicity over this. Clay's death will be in the papers again," he said, his voice quiet, sorrowful.

She brushed the strand of hair behind her ear. "I know," she said in the same tone. She sighed. "I'm glad it's over."

Stephanie learned exactly how intrusive reporters could be during the next few days. Newspapers all over the country made a big deal out of the arrests of the ex-cop and the businessman, the setup with the other robberies, then the double-cross as the man stashed the necklace without sharing any of the insurance proceeds with his partner in crime.

Television stations picked up the story and swarmed over the town. Stephanie gave three interviews, then declined any others. She and Nick were declared heroes for figuring the case out. The insurance company paid them a percentage of the necklace's value for recovery of fraud. She put her share of the money in a college fund for Doogie. Nick quietly donated his to the county youth program.

"Now I know where the expression 'a three-day wonder' came from," Pat remarked with a rather sarcastic smirk at the end of the week following all the excitement. "The press was all over the place for three days, then they packed up and left like a plague of locusts heading for the next pasture."

"Some crackpot tried to shoot the mayor in some town in Texas." Amy, as a small town mayor's wife, looked worried.

"No one will shoot our mayor," Pat assured her.

"You never know—" Amy broke off and studied

Stephanie, who had continued to add items to one of the
bargain baskets during the conversation.

Stephanie glanced up with an understanding smile.
"It's okay. *I'm* okay."

Her friends and neighbors were eager to talk about the
case, but they didn't want to remind her of her loss. She
appreciated their kindness. It was truly over now, and the
past could be laid to rest.

She sighed and gazed out the window toward the mountains. For some reason those lofty peaks, so far above it
all, gave her solace. She didn't understand how people
who had grown up near the towering peaks of the Rockies
could bear to live out of sight of these fierce sentinels.

"It's time for us to close," Amy said.

Stephanie checked the time. Noon. They were all to go
to a wedding at two o'clock, so they were closing the
store early today. Nick's brother, the minister, was getting
married.

For a while everyone had thought he would marry the
organist at church, but she'd married someone else. Geoff
was marrying a woman he'd met at the resort and known
for a total of three months. The Dorelli boys had always
had a reputation for reckless behavior....

She said goodbye and hurried out to her car, leaving
first, as her home was the farthest away.

The air was crisp with the promise of fall. September.
She loved the change of seasons. By the end of the month
the leaves would be in full color.

A time of change.

She considered the possibilities while she dressed for
the wedding. A time *for* change, she decided.

Stephanie hummed as she slipped into a blue linen suit
with a printed silk blouse. She brushed her hair into a
smooth bob that ended in a blunt cut even with her chin.

She'd gotten it cut to the shorter length yesterday. Her hair had grown quite a bit during the summer. She'd been so busy she hadn't had it trimmed in ages. She felt odd not having it brush her shoulders.

She finished her preparations and checked her purse for her car keys before heading out the door. Doogie was at Clyde's house where he was spending the night along with several others. A slumber party. Although boys didn't call them that.

"A sleepover," Doogie had corrected her with righteous indignation. "Only girls have slumber parties." This last had been uttered with total disgust.

She smiled. He was noticing the opposite sex.

As she backed and turned out of her drive, she realized she was humming a song from her own brief wedding. The minister's wife had played the piano for them.

At the church, she found Pat had saved her a seat.

"You look melancholy," her friend remarked.

"I was thinking of my wedding on the way here," Stephanie confessed. "Thirteen years ago. A lifetime."

"Not so long. You're still young." Pat nudged her side. "Here comes Nick. Slide over, and we'll make room for him. His family pew is full."

Stephanie had no choice but to follow Pat's example as she slid closer to her neighbor. Nick slipped onto the padded bench beside her. He wore a suit rather than his uniform. The last time she'd seen him so attired had been at Amy's Christmas party.

Christmas was three months and twenty-six days away.

Her lips became warmer, softer with the remembered pressure of his mouth on hers. Once she'd adored him. When she'd been a girl. My, she was feeling melancholy today.

When she saw Nick watching her, she smiled at him,

a slow, deliberate smile of welcome. Like the seasons, it was time for a change between them, too.

He gave her a brief but intense stare, then looked away without returning her smile. He'd avoided her during the hoopla over the burglary. The fresh scent of his cologne filled her nostrils as she drew a deep breath.

From the corner of her eye, she could see the bony ridges of his face and the clean-shaven appearance he presented. He wasn't as handsome as Clay had been, but there was something deeply compelling in the harsher planes of his face. It was as if he'd been created at the same time the dark granite of the mountains had surged upward toward the heavens, as if his eyes had been forged in the dark fires of volcanic tumult, like the black obsidian shards she found along the creek.

She sensed a quiet sadness in him. He'd been right. The story of Clay's death had been enacted every night on TV after the police had found the necklace in a safety deposit box at a Denver bank. Not even the man's wife had known he had it. The necklace had been an heirloom from her side of the family.

So the case was solved and the perpetrators were in jail. It was time to put the past, all of it, behind them. Life went on.

Pat leaned across her. "Hi, Nick. Where have you been keeping yourself? I haven't seen you at the diner in an age."

He turned toward the two women. Stephanie's heart gave a hitch when he looked at her. All the Dorellis had beautiful eyes set off by the longest, blackest lashes. She gazed at her hands, folded in her lap, waiting for her heart to settle down.

"I've been riding the county roads out toward the ranch for the past few days. I rotated back to town last week."

The sheriff's department handled the town's law enforcement needs, too. The deputies took turns patrolling the various areas—a small force to keep law and order over a large area.

"How are things with the store? Did the Labor Day sale go okay?" he asked politely.

There was a beat of silence. Stephanie glanced up and saw he was looking at her. "Yes, it was fine." A crystal radiance bloomed in her. She felt as if she had champagne instead of blood circulating in her body.

"I saw Doogie taking care of the sidewalk items."

"Yes. He wanted to earn some extra money."

"That's good. A kid learns the value of a dollar when he has to work for it."

"You're absolutely right," she said, sounding as if she were in a dream, even to herself.

Pat's eyebrows rose in amusement. Stephanie tried to stem the tide of sparkling blood that rushed to her face. She was in danger of making a fool of herself. She didn't care.

"Sorry," Nick said quietly. "I didn't mean anything. I was making conversation." He smiled, his teeth a startling white against his tanned skin. "I'll shut up."

"That's okay. You were right before about Doogie needing to be with boys his age. He did. He likes working, too. It seems to be good for him."

Beside her, Pat gave a snort of laughter. Stephanie ignored it. Instead, she focused on the tantalizing outline of Nick's mouth. His lips were rather thin, but soft and mobile when he used them on a person....

She almost moaned aloud. Carefully she drew another breath, taking in his scent with the cool fall air. She felt surrounded by his overpowering maleness. Her lungs tried to quit functioning. Dizziness rolled over her in a hazy cloud. She thought she might faint. Right into his arms, of course.

The ceremony began. When the bride came down the aisle in a froth of white satin, she couldn't stop the tears that formed. Once she had been young and full of dreams.

She still was. The knowledge came over her with the quietness of a whisper, a comforting conviction that life still held dreams and surprises and good things. For a long time she'd had all the care and none of the delight of living.

It *was* time for a change. She glanced outside at the cottonwood leaves trembling in the gentle wind.

Nick moved, his shoulder brushing hers as he resettled in his seat. The touch went through her like heat lightning. He glanced over at her and, seeing her gaze, gave her a long, thoughtful perusal as if he couldn't quite figure her out.

She smiled beatifically at him.

He frowned and set his gaze on the front of the church where his brother was taking his vows under the direction of a minister friend who had gone to seminary with him. Stephanie watched and listened to the proceedings with a deep sense of satisfaction.

Life moved along at its merry pace.

When the bride and groom rushed up the aisle, she stood with the rest of the congregation. Her shoulder brushed Nick's. She leaned into him a bit before straightening. He gave her a suspicious glance. She gave him another smile.

"Are you going straight over to the reception?" Pat asked.

"Yes—"

"Yes—"

She and Nick answered together. He gestured for her to speak first.

"Do you want a ride?" she asked Pat.

"If you don't mind. I walked over. My car is in the shop. As usual." She rolled her eyes.

"You might think of something more practical for the area next time you trade," Nick suggested.

"That'll be about a hundred years from now," Pat wailed in mock sorrow. She had a classic European car.

The person across the way brushed against Stephanie as she stepped into the aisle. Nick clasped her elbow.

She tucked her arm close to her body and felt his fingers against her side, close to her breast.

His eyes narrowed as she sighed. "Sorry," he said. He stepped aside and made room for her and Pat to exit their row.

Pat gave her an odd glance before turning to Nick, her light gray eyes bright and inviting as the three made their way slowly toward the bride and groom at the door. "Maybe I'll ask your help in selecting a new car if I ever decide to get rid of the old one."

"Sure." He gave his brother a hearty slap on the back and kissed the bride on her cheek before stepping outside the door. "Excuse me." He strode over to the sheriff, who was talking to the mayor.

"Well, talk about being left at the church door," Pat remarked as she and Stephanie headed down the steps after the customary kisses and greetings. She laughed, her eyes following Nick's tall form as he joined the other two men. "They seem rather serious about something."

Stephanie glanced at the side lawn. Nick was nodding his head in understanding at something the sheriff was saying. He looked very serious.

He was rarely the devil-may-care young man she'd

fallen in love with so many years ago. She wanted to hear him laugh again. She wanted happiness for him.

She and Pat chatted idly on the way to the Dorelli ranch for the reception. The family was one of the oldest in these parts. There was to be a buffet dinner, then dancing until the wee hours. Presumably the bride and groom would be long gone before the party was over.

Her own wedding party had consisted of her mother and Clay's mom and two brothers.

"If I ever get married, I think I'll choose a rich man. Look at the size of this house," Pat whispered as they approached the open front door.

The Dorelli house wasn't a mansion, but a ranch house with a wing that had been added when the family had increased. Lupe, who'd been cook there since the dark ages, was busily putting platter after platter of goodies on a huge sideboard.

One of her nieces directed them to the patio where there were ten tables, each set with eight place settings of china and silver on pink linen tablecloths. She was relieved there were no place cards. With luck, Nick would be seated beside her.

A dance pavilion occupied center place on the lawn. Good. Nick liked to dance. So did she.

Amy gestured them over to her. "I've saved seats for all of us," she confided. "Here, Stephanie, sit there. Pat, take that chair. I've invited the new deputy you were ogling the other day at the diner to join us."

The mayor strolled over with Nick and the sheriff five minutes later. The new man was with them. Amy directed the men to their chairs.

Nick was placed on Stephanie's right with the new man to her left and Pat on the other side of him.

"Have you met Jack Karew?" Nick asked the women.

"No. Hello, Jack. I'm pleased to meet you," Stephanie said.

"Jack, this is Stephanie Bolt. She and Amy own the Glass Slipper Boutique on Main Street. Pat, here, works there."

"I've met Pat," the new deputy said and shook hands with each of the women. He turned to Stephanie. "Bolt. There was a deputy by that name, I recall—"

"My husband," she said quickly, but pleasantly. "Isn't this a lovely place? It's just perfect for watching twilight creep over the hills."

"Yes," Nick agreed. His voice had the most soothing qualities—deep and quiet, as if the world was a safe place because he was in it. Clay had once commented on Nick's ability to calm people down in a stressful situation.

Guests continued to arrive until finally everyone was there, including the bride and groom and their family, who had finished the photo session. A local photographer snapped candid shots of the party, some of them Polaroid pictures for the guests to take home with them. "Very thoughtful," Stephanie commented.

Nick leaned over her shoulder to gaze at a photo of their group. "Yes."

Stephanie felt his breath on her neck. She met his gaze and felt an electrical current race away into the depths of her. She reached for her champagne glass in self-defense, to stop herself from reaching for him.

His quiet ways contrasted sharply with the dark fire that suddenly seemed to glow in his eyes.

"A toast," the best man exclaimed. That was Joseph, the oldest of the four Dorelli boys. Standing, he delivered with grave seriousness several stories regarding the groom that couldn't possibly be true. They drank to each one.

The father of the bride proposed a toast to the couple.

They drank to that. Then the bride's brother warned the groom about the length of time she spent primping in the bathroom.

"I suspect the groom knows her habits very well," the mayor muttered, raising his glass in the toast. "Well, maybe not," he added with an apologetic glance at Nick after recalling the groom was a minister and the deputy's brother.

"Shh," Amy whispered.

Nick's father welcomed the bride's parents into their family. They lifted their glasses to his toast. He spoke for ten minutes on the joys and responsibilities of marriage, bringing tears to the women's eyes. Mr. Dorelli had married his bookkeeper four years ago, shocking the entire community at this surprising event.

The glasses were refilled as the convivial toasts proceeded through the relatives.

Nick stood. "To the bride and groom." They drank to that. "And the grandchildren my father thinks he's entitled to."

Stephanie laughed with the crowd as the bride turned suitably pink. The groom chuckled, too.

"And to Nonna, who will tell you how to raise them," he added.

The chipper grandmother, who was closing in on a hundred years of age, nodded graciously. Nikki, Nick's charming niece, nestled close to the old woman. Nikki's mom discreetly nursed the new baby while her father watched his family with a loving gleam in his eyes that were as blue as his daughter's.

They were a nice family, these Dorellis and their kin.

Heat spread slowly through Stephanie as the evening wore on. Happiness bubbled through her. She found everything amusing.

"Watch the champagne," Nick warned at one point. "It can be potent if you're not used to it, especially at this altitude."

"I'm perfectly fine," she retorted, then grinned at him.

He gazed at her, his mood solemn. Finally he smiled and shook his head as if giving up on telling her how to behave.

"You have the most engaging smile," she told him. "I've noticed before."

"Have you now," he murmured. His gaze flicked over her in a questioning perusal. There was a wariness in his attitude toward her. She'd have to do something about it.

She batted her eyelashes at him, then arched her back and preened under his keen, appreciative study. He had a way of looking at a person as if he really saw them. She liked that.

After the cake was cut and everyone had had a chance to eat as much as they liked, the bride and groom started the dancing. The bride's father cut in. The groom led his mother onto the floor. Mr. Dorelli danced with the bride's mother.

"It's so elegant and romantic," Stephanie whispered, feeling the tears gather once more. "The way a wedding should be."

"Let's dance," Amy said to her husband when other couples drifted to the floor.

"Yes, let's." Nick stood and looked down at her.

Stephanie felt herself being drawn to her feet by his strong hand on her arm. She followed him to the dance pavilion in a dreamy haze. Tahiti torches ringed the floor, adding light and warmth as the evening cooled and a mountain breeze sprang up.

The moon, a silver arc of light, balanced on the tip of

a nearby peak. Stephanie shivered at how beautiful it all was.

Nick pulled her closer into his arms. His warmth surrounded her like a cocoon of golden silk. She laid her head on his shoulder and sighed contentedly.

Lips feathered lightly along her temple. "Mmm," she crooned. She linked her arms around his neck and closed her eyes.

"Don't go to sleep, Steph," Nick whispered close to her ear. He sounded worried.

"I'm not," she assured him. "The night is young, and there are other things we can do...."

"Shh," he said.

She ignored his caution. "We can make love."

Chapter Ten

"Dammit," Nick muttered. He pulled her tight against him.

Stephanie smiled as desire grew between them. He held himself rigid. She wasn't so restrained. She kissed his jaw, then the corner of his frowning mouth before settling her head once more into the groove of his shoulder. Ah, perfect.

Her conscience scolded her for taunting him, but her thoughts blurred as soon as they formed, like wispy clouds flying across the moon.

"Let's go home, Nick." She yawned delicately.

"That's the only sensible thing I've heard from you tonight."

"Don't be angry."

"I'm not," he said in a deeper, quieter tone.

She tried to look him squarely in the eye, but each time she did she thought she might drown or burn up in the liquid fire in those depths. "This is too confusing."

"It's simple," he insisted. "Very simple. You're drunk."

That was funny. "Am not," she contradicted. Except maybe drunk on love. His arm closed around her shoulder, and she snuggled against that solid pillow of warmth again. She wanted to stay there. "Umm," she said happily.

"I'm taking her home," Nick said. "She's had enough. Would you drive her car home? I'll arrange to pick it up tomorrow."

Stephanie opened her eyes. Pat nodded and took the keys Nick offered. "Is she all right?" she asked.

"Yeah, nothing a good night's sleep won't fix."

"I may go to bed, but I won't go to sleep," Stephanie announced with great dignity.

Nick gave her an exasperated glance, then led her from the house. She said good-night to his sister when they passed and to his grandmother, who was about as tall as a gremlin and looked rather like a friendly one.

She was humming when Nick put her in the cruiser.

He was cursing.

She sang snatches of love songs all the way to the house. There, Nick helped her down from the truck and into the house as if she were an invalid. "Where's Doogie?"

"Clyde's. A sleepover." She dropped her suit jacket over a kitchen chair, her shoes by the door, her blouse over the doorknob—

"Will you cut that out?" Nick snapped behind her.

"What?" She couldn't figure out what he was getting all steamed about. They had the house and the night to themselves.

"Undressing everywhere in the house. Go to your bedroom."

"Yes, sir," she said meekly.

He followed along behind, her discarded clothing in hand. He placed her jacket and blouse on a chair, her shoes beneath it. "I'd better go."

"Stay."

Silence greeted her invitation. "I can't," he finally said.

"Please." It would spoil everything if he left.

"I can't. Not tonight. You...we're too vulnerable."

She noticed he'd included himself. "Good," she murmured. She stripped out of her skirt and tossed it toward the chair. She missed, but Nick caught it and laid it neatly over the other items. She gave him an approving smile.

He ran a hand through his hair. "Steph, don't. Whatever you're doing, just...don't, you hear?"

"What am I doing?" She sat down on the bed and pulled her nightgown from under the pillow. It wasn't cotton. Instead she'd substituted a satin and lace confection Amy had ordered for the shop. She'd bought one for herself.

"Driving me crazy," he said with a snarl. He stalked toward her. "Let's get you in bed so I can get out of here. Do you need to go to the bathroom?"

She couldn't help it. She giggled. "I'm not your niece," she reminded him.

He wiped sweat from his brow. "I sure as hell know that. Nikki isn't a brat."

"And I am?" She tried to sound indignant, but a gurgle of laughter escaped.

"You're a menace, that's what you are. Get this gown on and get in bed. Now."

She couldn't bring herself to taunt him more. She went into the bathroom, changed into the frothy gown and pulled on the matching peignoir before returning to the bedroom.

Nick stood by the bed. He'd folded the covers back and was waiting to tuck her in. His expression was grim, that of a condemned man who was determined to die with honor. Her mood became solemn as she studied his beloved face.

She wanted so much for him—happiness and love and all the desires of his heart. She prayed desperately that she was one of those desires. She wanted to be.

"Nick," she said, his name drawn from her soul as she went to him.

"Get in bed, Steph," he ordered sternly. "You've had too much champagne."

She sat on the side of the bed and put her arms around his lean waist. She rested her head against him and heard the strong, steady beating of his heart. Their love would have been like that, strong and enduring, if it had ever had a chance to mature.

The loss of all the years they could have shared stretched backward in time like a dark unending highway. The future seemed the same. Unless they did something to change it. A keen ache pierced all the way through her heart.

She tightened her hold on him. "Stay," she whispered against his shirt, loving the warmth radiating from beneath the material, needing that warmth as part of herself, wanting to give her heat to him.

"Steph," he said. It was a protest and a groan of need. "Stay."

His hands gripped her shoulders. She leaned her head back and gazed up at him, pleading, desperate. She sensed that something precious would be lost for all time if this moment was allowed to pass unheeded.

"Don't," he said, his voice rough with anger. "Damn you, don't look at me like that."

"Like what?"

"Like you'll die if I don't kiss you." He sounded as desperate as she had.

"No, I won't die, but my life will be infinitely sadder."

His breath hissed between his tightly clenched teeth as he locked his hands into fistfuls of her hair and pushed her head against him. Slowly he combed his fingers through the strands, smoothing them as if he sought comfort from the act.

"Steph." This time the word was an admission of need and hunger mixed with anger and doubt.

A potent brew of emotions.

She stroked her hands over his back, pulled his shirt free and ran her hands under it, touching his warm skin. "You feel so good. Oh, Nick, you feel so very, very good."

Nick pressed his hands along her back to her waist, running his thumbs along her spine, loving the feel of her bones under his touch. She was delicate compared to a man's brawn, yet with a strength that matched his in this contest of give and take.

Her eyes were dreamy and filled with promises that a hungry man wanted to hear. Muscles tightened, flesh expanded. No amount of reasoning on his part could penetrate the aura of need that encircled him, enclosing him in her magic.

She was the love of his youth, the flame he was forever drawn to through the darkness of time and years and denial.

Slowly he let his weight bow over her, pressing her lightly. She fell onto the bed as if in slow motion, each inch taking an agony of time, until she at last rested against the mattress. He let himself down beside her.

Her eyelashes reclined at half mast, but they didn't hide

the glow of desire in her eyes as she gazed at him. She touched his jaw, his cheek, then smoothed the lock of hair from his forehead. She was a woman asking for what he wanted to give.

"Ah, Steph," he breathed, letting his full length fit itself to her soft curves.

He slipped one thigh between hers. Heat folded around him, causing him to grimace as muscles tightened and flexed in a spasm of need too great to deny. He had to be in the very center of that heat, in the very center of that softness.

She was all cool satin and warm skin, pale silk and rosy flesh, dark curls and sun-kissed locks. And she was his.

The pulse at her temple was erratic, flickering like a tiny beast trying to escape. He kissed her there, then proceeded down her face to the mole that so enticed him. He circled it with his tongue and felt her move against him. Heat blasted through him like a furnace.

Unable to prolong the play, he took her lips, melding his to hers, seeking the inside of her mouth with his tongue, feeling her respond with no hesitation, opening to him, taking him in, returning every caress.

It was heaven and hell and everything in between, to hold her like this and know she was his for the taking. He had only to strip the clothes from them and the night would be theirs.

Wild, sweet torment. Wild, sweet pleasure.

He moved against her, his body mimicking the message of his tongue as the kiss went on and on, growing hotter, needier, with every second. She sighed, caught her breath and held it for an alarming time, then sighed again.

Her nipples puckered against the nightgown. He stroked them through the satin, making little circles around and around each areola until she grabbed his hand and laid it over her breast and squeezed, showing him what she wanted. He massaged and stroked over the whole surface. She made little murmurs of delight that set off fireworks in his blood.

She was his...for this moment.

He shook his head slightly. He didn't want to think beyond the here and now. The present was all that mattered. There was no past, no future, just *now* and the sweet mindless pleasure of the senses.

"Love me," she urged, her hands restless on his skin. She unfastened his shirt and ran her nails through the whorls of hair on his chest. "Oh, Nick, it's been so long. Make love to me."

He shuddered as her longing pierced the shield around his heart. He had loved her all those years ago, and God help him but he loved her now. He had only to claim her....

Once she'd looked at him with this very same loving light in her eyes, but in the end she'd gone to another man. No matter how they'd parted—and he knew he'd been at fault as much or more than she had—still the results were the same. She'd said she loved him, but she'd married another.

The memory beat through the haze of passion. Her hands at his belt propelled him to action. He pulled away from her. She murmured in protest. When she would have followed him, he caught her hands and pinned them on the bed above her head.

"No, Steph," he ground out. It hurt, saying those words. The denial of needs so long withheld ached like a broken tooth.

She opened her eyes—beautiful, slumberous eyes, eyes so blue he felt as if he were drowning whenever he gazed into them—and watched him in puzzlement. There was aching protest in those depths. She wanted him now, this instant. That was clear.

And heaven help him, he wanted her, this woman, this love of his life.... "This is champagne talk. Women always get sentimental at weddings. Tomorrow you'd regret anything that happened tonight." He drew a ragged breath, need fighting with doubt, wanting to believe everything he saw in her eyes, but unable to cast aside the cynicism of the past.

"No." She brushed her fingers through his hair. "I want you, only you."

"Be sure, Steph. There'll be no going back."

She moved restlessly against him. "I am sure," she murmured in a reproving tone, "but you aren't."

When she pushed upright, he moved to the end of the bed while she propped her back against the pillows.

She moved her head slowly from side to side. "There has to be trust, Nick. When you can give me yours without reservations, then come to me and I'll be yours... forever, if you want me. It's something you'll have to decide—love and trust and a future, or nothing. Which will it be?"

With an ache like that of an old man in the marrow of his bones, Nick listened to her quiet demand. The need to be in her was so great he almost gave in to his body's demand for fulfillment and to hell with anything else. He knew he could overcome her protests and claim her.

And then what?

The doubts ate at him. He could lie and say he didn't have any qualms about their future, he could probably convince her the doubts didn't matter, but she would know, and so would he. "What if I don't return?"

Her breath caught, then she released it slowly. "Then

it's better to know. If you really can't trust me, we're better off apart than living with doubt between us."

He nodded. Pain lanced through him as he watched the fire die in her eyes. She was so beautiful and so determined to have love on her terms.

He buttoned his shirt. He paused as the longing hit him again, then he shook his head. "You ask for a lot."

Stephanie bit back the words that tried to escape her lips. She experienced a vague sense of finality. She'd offered herself and her love to him. He'd rejected them.

She hugged her knees to her chest. The lovely satin peignoir spread out around her, an invitation of pleasure to the senses. A sigh worked its way from deep inside her. She'd been terribly vain. She'd thought she only needed to tempt Nick into her arms and he would confess undying love. It was a lesson in humility.

"I want a lot," she confessed.

He stood, and she realized he really was going to leave. She'd been wrong. She'd thought they were falling in love all over again, but it was obvious only she was in love. If Nick truly loved her, he would trust her.

She managed a smile. "Thank you for your help with Doogie and for clearing Clay's name. I hope you find happiness. You deserve it more than anyone I've ever known."

A pained expression darted over his handsome face before a wry smile appeared. "That sounds like one of those 'damned with faint praise' remarks."

"I mean it. I hope you find the woman who will make your dreams come true, one you can trust with the love I know you're capable of giving."

"I once thought you were that woman." He lingered for another second, his eyes dark as bitter chocolate, his thoughts unreadable as he studied her. Then he walked out.

She listened to his footsteps die away, then the sounds of his truck starting and the tires crunching on the gravel.

The quiet settled like dust on a dying breeze. She stayed where she was for a long time, as if she were waiting for something. The clock ticked, the wind blew, the dawn crawled over the horizon and still she waited.

Stephanie handed the balance sheet to Amy. "That was one of the best quarters we've ever had."

"Yes, it was. I'm so glad we started this place. It's been fun, hasn't it?" Amy studied the figures. When she looked up, her expression was somber. "You've been quiet of late."

Stephanie nodded. "I've been thinking." She smiled.

"What about?"

"Life. Truth. Beauty. All the important questions."

"Hmm, heavy thinking. Any conclusions?"

"Not a one." She sighed and turned her gaze toward the mountain visible through the barred window of the office. Not only her thoughts were heavy. Her soul was, too.

"Is it Nick?"

She swung a startled gaze to her partner. "Nick?"

"Yes. Are you in love with him?"

Stephanie smiled ruefully. "Terribly."

"You two were once a couple."

"A long time ago."

"Not so long. What about when he took you home after the wedding? There were fireworks between you two. Even my husband could see it, and he's usually oblivious to anything not on the front page of the *Post*."

"Nick put me to bed and walked out."

Amy's brows rose in disbelief. "The boy is sick."

Steph shook her head. "He thinks I betrayed him. Only he can decide if he trusts my love enough to try again. So far he doesn't."

"He said that?" Amy rolled her eyes heavenward. "He's a fool, a blind fool, if he can't see what you two have."

Stephanie put the balance sheet back in the file and closed it. She filed the report in the file cabinet and locked it. "That's it for today. Time to go home."

Home would be an empty house. Doogie and the debate team had gone to a competition in Denver on the school bus. They would be gone overnight.

"Why don't you come home with me? We're going to grill some steaks. Our neighbors, the Almons, are coming over. You know them. She works at the drugstore."

"No, thanks, Amy. I have chores to do at home. Thanks all the same." Stephanie gathered her purse and jacket. She said good night and let herself out the back door.

In her car, zipping along the county road a few minutes later, she let her gaze roam over the mountains. The aspen on the higher slopes and the cottonwoods along the creek trembled in shades of buttery gold. The plate-leaf maples were russet and scarlet. October had settled gently into Indian summer.

So far the weather had held steady—warm days, crisp nights, a bit of frost to glitter in the morning sunlight.

The store was doing much better than they'd expected, even with this being the slow time for tourists. Things were going well at home, too.

Doogie was a good student and treasurer of his class this year. He was taking gymnastics at Nick's suggestion to increase his balance and overall tone. The money from the fall sale of calves had paid for a new roof.

She should be at peace.

She was. Really. Her life was as smooth as hot fudge. As long as she avoided the subject of Nick Dorelli. She'd hardly gotten a glimpse of him during the past three days. In a small town, it was impossible to avoid anyone completely. There were only so many places to go.

The sound of her sigh broke into her musing. She frowned and proceeded to give herself a stern lecture on life and love and the hazards that go with those elements.

She slowed at a sharp curve. Almost home. She'd change and do the chores before dark descended—

A car came around the curve. It was upon her almost as soon as she saw it. She instinctively swung the wheel hard to the right. Her tires dropped off the pavement onto the gravel.

She heard the squealing of tires as the other driver tried to hold his vehicle to the inside of the curve. But he'd taken the curve way too fast. He was in the outside lane. There was no place for her to go but over the edge of the steep hill.

Her compact vehicle bounced wildly as it careered across a shallow ditch, then down the tree-shrouded slope. Trees hit it from both sides. Stopping was impossible. Gravity had taken over. She heard glass breaking, then gasped as a huge oak loomed in front of her. Her last thought before the crash was that the tree would at least stop the fall....

A cloud appeared before her eyes. She realized what it was when the air bag hit her in the face.

Nick was nearing the Bolt ranch when he got a call about a car being off the road near there. He was less than a mile from the site. He told the dispatcher he'd handle it. He flipped on the flashing rack of police lights and speeded up.

Nick took in the situation at a glance when he arrived at the skid marks. The driver had evidently been going too fast to make the curve. Probably some kid.

After parking in a turnout, he set out flares up and down the highway to warn other motorists of trouble. He attached a rope to the bumper of the cruiser, stuck a flashlight and first aid kit into his gun belt and started down the steep slope.

The path of the vehicle was easy to follow. It had cut a swath through the saplings and come to a halt against an old oak. A limb had broken off and covered most of the car.

He ducked under the branches and got a good look at the car. His heart stopped, then pounded fiercely. He wrenched open the battered door. "Steph," he said, his throat so tight he could hardly get her name out.

She pushed upright off the steering wheel. Blood ran from her nose and soaked her blouse. "Nick?"

He laid a hand on her shoulder. "Don't move. I want to check you over."

"I'm all right."

He snorted. He shook out a white handkerchief. "Here. Your nose is bleeding."

She pulled the visor down. "Good heavens."

"Yeah, right," he agreed. He checked her legs and feet. "Move your foot," he ordered. "Does that hurt?"

"No. Really, I'm okay. The air bag saved me. Except for my nose. I think it broke when I hit the thing."

"Why the hell were you driving so fast?" He released the seat belt and pushed it aside.

"I wasn't. There was another car. It rounded the curve on my side and forced me off the road."

He pulled the lever and let the seat back. "Okay, let's get you out of here. Did you happen to get his tag number?" he asked with wry humor.

"No, it was a red sports car with white pinstriping on the side." The corners of her mouth turned up on each side of the hankie she had pressed to her nose.

Something tender warred with the anger he'd felt upon seeing her in the wreck. He fought an impulse to gather her into his arms and take her home with him. He might let her out on her own in a hundred years.

Watch it, he warned. The adrenaline was running high right now. It could cause a man to do stupid things.

"Come on," he ordered gruffly. "Let's get you to the emergency room. I'll call the garage for a tow truck."

"Thank you." She smiled sweetly at him, then swayed.

He caught her before she hit the ground. She wasn't totally out, but she was in shock, a leftover from the excitement of nearly getting herself killed. He cursed softly, reining in his temper with an effort.

When he'd seen her head down and blood all over, he'd thought...never mind what he'd thought. He had to get her out of here. It would be dark in an hour. The air was already on the chilly side.

"Sorry," she murmured. "I'm okay now."

"I'll be the judge of that. Get in front of me. We'll walk out together."

He placed her in front of him and used the rope to pull them up the steep slope, enclosing her in his arms as he did. Her hair rubbed against his chin, and her behind bumped against his groin as they climbed. The anger caused by fear turned into a raging lust. He clenched his teeth on a groan.

They reached the road at last. He lifted her into the

cruiser, set out a couple more flares and flicked the lights on when he headed for town.

"You again?" The doctor laughed as he bent over Stephanie. He glanced at Nick. "Good thing she has you around to rescue her, eh, Nick?" He seemed to think the whole thing funny.

Stephanie flinched when the doctor peered up her nose. He decided to put in a new gadget to hold the cartilage in place while her nose healed.

"There, that should fix you right up. You're going to have a couple of shiners. Use an ice pack for the next forty-eight hours to keep the swelling down. I'll give you a shot so you can sleep tonight."

After the treatment and filling out a dozen forms for the insurance plus filing a police report with Nick, she was at last dismissed.

"I'll take you home," Nick volunteered. "Where's Doogie?"

"Denver with the debate team. They're spending the night." She yawned when they were in the truck once more.

"Don't go to sleep," he told her.

"I think you said that when I broke my arm."

She remembered how gentle he'd been as he'd helped her into the house. He'd almost undressed her. She swallowed as tears filled her throat. She'd missed having him around the past couple of weeks. He'd avoided her, too. Of course she'd seen him around town. That couldn't be helped, but it was only glimpses, not enough to satisfy her need for him.

The love that had bloomed when first they'd started dating had lain dormant during the long winter of their separation. Now it bloomed again in her heart, fiery and wild and disturbing.

He stopped at her house. "Are you crying?" he asked, peering through the twilight at her.

She shook her head. That made her nose hurt. "No."

He snorted, but said nothing more. He helped her out, setting her on her feet so gently she didn't feel a jolt. In the house he guided her to the bedroom, retrieved her gown and handed it to her. Then he left.

Fighting the useless emotion, she removed her clothing, keeping her balance by holding on to the bed post, and tried to slip the gown over her head without touching her nose.

Hands covered hers and a strong chest was suddenly there for her to lean against. Nick eased the gown over her head and onto each arm, one of his arms around her waist. His hand sizzled against her bare skin.

"Nick," she said in a wobbly voice.

"Shh, let's get you tucked in." He stripped the covers back and urged her into bed. Then he pulled the sheet up to her chin. From the night table he picked up an ice pack and laid it carefully across her face.

She didn't like it. "I can't see you," she protested.

"You don't need to see me."

"Yes, I do." She removed the pack and stared at his beloved face. He was so handsome and wonderful and...everything. She got choked up thinking about it.

"You're crying," he muttered. He spun away and disappeared from her view.

He returned in less than a minute with a cool cloth. He wiped her face and laid it over her eyes, then replaced the ice pack. "Keep this in place."

"Don't go away," she whispered. Her throat ached as well as her nose. The pain killer the doctor had given her was taking effect. She could feel herself slipping toward oblivion just as her car had slipped out of her control heading down the hill. "Hold my hand."

He took her hand in his. She scooted over so he could sit on the bed. She felt his thigh touch hers, then his warmth through the blanket and sheet.

"Stay," she pleaded. "Please stay."

"I'll be here." There was a thread of sardonic amusement in his tone.

"Promise?" She waited anxiously during the long pause.

"Promise."

She sighed and let herself slide on into sleep.

At ten Nick eased his hand free, pulled up a chair and sat beside Stephanie while she slept. He noted the picture of Clay was gone. There was no ring on her finger. He stared at the empty space in the queen-size bed. That space should have been his. He should have the right to sleep there and hold her during the night when she became restless with pain.

He wanted that right, no matter that another man had had it first. It should have been his....

Grim with needs and thoughts he couldn't control, he found a blanket in the closet. Kicking his shoes aside, he propped his feet on the bed next to Steph's—that way he would feel her shift during the night—spread the blanket over himself and closed his eyes. He awoke every hour and checked the ice pack. At midnight and at four, he replaced the melted ice with fresh chips.

The dawn was a long time in coming. He was stiff when he woke for the last time. It was eight o'clock. Steph still slept like a baby.

He studied her before he rose. She looked young and innocent with her short honey-streaked hair tousled on the pillow. One foot stuck out from the covers. He touched it, then cupped it in his hand. Her toes were small and round rather than long and bony as his were.

He loved a barefoot woman.

The thought drew an involuntary smile. He'd gone off the deep end, but it didn't seem to matter. He bent his head and kissed the delicate arch of her foot, then along her ankle.

He stroked the instep and felt her flinch. He remembered she was ticklish there and on her ribs. So many things to remember. They'd missed out on large parts of life, but they'd shared a lot, too.

Thinking this over, he covered her foot and headed for the shower. Thirty minutes later he entered the bedroom again. She stirred when he set the tray down.

"Breakfast," he announced when she opened her eyes.

"That looks wonderful. I'm starved." She pushed up against the pillows.

He remembered her sitting there when he'd left her, her face composed, but her eyes sad. She'd wanted him to stay with her then, too. But he hadn't. He'd tucked his tail between his legs and lit out, afraid to take what she offered.

"I think we'd better have a talk," he said.

She darted a quick glance at him. "Okay." She slipped past him and went to the bathroom. He went for the coffee and a tray for himself. When he returned, she was in bed.

"You look awful," he told her, placing the tray across her lap. He grinned.

"How ungallant to say so."

"If I hadn't, you would've. I was saving you the trouble."

She tried to laugh, but ended up in a grimace of pain. "My nose hurts," she complained.

"Yeah, well, when you drive over cliffs..." He picked

up his fork and started eating the scrambled eggs and toast.

Steph ate when Nick did. She keep stealing glances at him. Something was different. She didn't know what. His eyes held a determined cast when he looked at her. She wished she had the right to throw herself in his arms, but she didn't.

"You spent the night," she commented as she spread jelly on her last piece of toast.

"Yeah. Your reputation is ruined."

She smiled. A little smile. It hurt to move her mouth much. "Thanks for rescuing me."

"It's my job."

"Is playing nursemaid also your job?"

"You needed someone with you."

A pang ricocheted through her chest, bouncing off her heart and ribs in a delicious tumult of sensation. She quelled her hopeless yearning. She'd been wrong before in her expectations for them. Nick was a caring person. She'd learned that from watching him with her son and the other boys. He probably felt sorry for her.

She caught sight of herself in the mirror on the dresser. Her eyes and nose were interesting shades of purple and green and swollen into a puffy blob.

When she finished, he took the trays away. She heard the water running in the kitchen while he cleaned up. She brushed her teeth gingerly, took an aspirin and went back to bed.

Nick returned and took the chair beside the bed. His face was grave, and his expression was the same as when he'd investigated Clay's involvement in the robbery. He was after the truth and nothing else would do.

She swallowed and cleared her throat twice.

Nick leaned forward with his forearms on his thighs and rubbed his hands together. He tried to think of some way to broach the subject he wanted to discuss. There was no other way except to just do it.

"Over the weekend you wanted me to stay with you," he began. "You weren't hurt then, but you'd been drinking champagne."

"Three glasses in a whole evening," she murmured.

He raised his head and looked at her directly, the level-eyed detective seeking the facts, just the facts, ma'am. She would have smiled, but it hurt too much.

"Did you know what you were doing?"

"Of course."

He frowned mightily at her. "Dammit, I'm serious, Steph."

"So am I. I wanted you to stay with me. I wanted you to sleep with me. Do you need it any plainer than that?"

He blinked once, shook his head, then changed his mind. "Yes. I need it a hell of a lot plainer than that."

"I hope you're not going to use that kind of language in front of our kids," she said, reprimanding him.

The next thing she knew he was in her face, his hands on her shoulders. He looked as fierce as a warrior out for blood, but his touch was so very gentle. "Listen, I'm sorry I walked out. I was being stubborn. As usual. I wanted to stay."

His voice was a hoarse murmur. She looked into his eyes and saw something like desperation and fear. This man, this strong, brave, caring man, was vulnerable... because of her.

Because he loved her. He had to. There was no other explanation. Her heart thumped like crazy.

She cupped his angular face in her hands. "I love you. I love you with a woman's love. I want to share my life with you, have children with you, grow old with you. I hope you want those things with me. I'm not an affair type person, Nick."

"God," he muttered. He closed his eyes.

"Don't say God unless you're talking to Him."

"I am. I'm praying I'm not dreaming." He leaned close, his face no more than a couple of inches from hers. "Am I, Steph? Am I dreaming you want me for a husband? You'd still take me after all that's happened?"

"Of course." She rubbed her thumbs along his hard jawbone.

"I couldn't forgive you for taking another in my place. That was stupid and selfish of me. I thought I'd be a fool to trust you again. I was a fool for ever doubting you. Will you forgive me? Will you be my love again?"

"Oh, darling, yes." She kissed him all over his face. "You were my very first, my very special love—"

"I want to be your last," he whispered fiercely. "I can take it that you loved another—a part of me will always regret the years we lost, but I can handle it. I love you, Steph. I've never stopped. You're the woman of my heart. You always have been. You always will be."

It was a promise so endearing she would have cried, except he didn't give her time. He took her mouth in the sweetest kiss she'd ever known. When they came up for air, she sighed happily. "No more stubborn silences from either of us. From now on, let's quarrel until we get everything settled."

"Right. We'll have regular shouting matches. Now, back to basics. How do you want to handle meals—take turns or you cook and I wash up?" At her astonished expression, he smiled. "My sister Dina says it's important to get all this ironed out before the wedding."

She laughed and tried to kiss him at the same time. They bumped noses. She yelped and covered her sore nose. "I am not becoming engaged looking like this," she declared.

Nick lay back on the bed and roared with laughter.

She listened and let the happiness seep down inside her. It was enough to fill a woman's heart to overflowing.

"I was on my way to your place when I got the call about your car being off the road," he said when he stopped laughing.

"You were?"

"Do you doubt it?" he demanded with a scowl.

"Yes. Uh, no. maybe you'd better convince me," she suggested, her gaze going to his sensuous mouth.

"I did some serious thinking about us and the past. A woman as loyal as you to her husband and their marriage, even when the going got tough, had to be true-blue. If that woman said she loved me, then who was I to argue with her about it?"

He gave her a solemn smile. His eyes asked forgiveness. She sighed contentedly. "A wise decision."

"The first of many. How many brothers are we going to give Doogie?"

"I'd like a girl."

"One boy and one girl," he countered. "Or two of each."

"Nick, we're thirty-four."

"Yeah. We'd better hurry. Let's get married next week."

"With me looking like this?" She started laughing.

He kissed her until she stopped. "To me you've always been the most beautiful woman alive."

She stroked through his thick, stubborn cowlick. "That must be true love."

"Yes." His eyes met hers, giving her a glimpse of heaven and a future filled with contentment.

"Yes," she agreed. And that said it all.

*　　*　　*　　*　　*

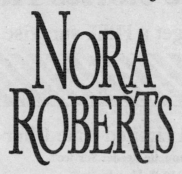

Take 4 bestselling love stories FREE

Plus get a FREE surprise gift!

DIANA WHITNEY

Continues the twelve-book
series 36 HOURS in
September 1997
with Book Three

OOH BABY, BABY

In the back of a cab, in the midst of a disastrous storm,
Travis Stockwell delivered Peggy Saxon's two precious babies
and, for a moment, they felt like a family. But Travis was a
wandering cowboy, and a fine woman like Peggy was better off
without him. Still, she and her adorable twins had tugged on
his heartstrings, until now he wasn't so sure that *he* was
better off without *her*.

For Travis and Peggy and *all* the residents of Grand Springs,
Colorado, the storm-induced blackout was just the beginning
of 36 Hours that changed *everything!* You won't want to miss a
single book.

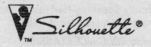

SILHOUETTE WOMEN KNOW ROMANCE WHEN THEY SEE IT.

And they'll see it on **ROMANCE CLASSICS**, the new 24-hour TV channel devoted to romantic movies and original programs like the special **Romantically Speaking-Harlequin® Goes Prime Time**.

Romantically Speaking-Harlequin® Goes Prime Time introduces you to many of your favorite romance authors in a program developed exclusively for Harlequin® and Silhouette® readers.

Watch for **Romantically Speaking-Harlequin® Goes Prime Time** beginning in the summer of 1997.

If you're not receiving ROMANCE CLASSICS, call your local cable operator or satellite provider and ask for it today!

Escape to the network of your dreams.

ROMANCE CLASSICS

You've been waiting for him all your life....
Now your Prince has finally arrived!

In fact, *three* handsome princes
are coming your way in

ROYAL WEDDINGS

A delightful new miniseries by **LISA KAYE LAUREL**
about three bachelor princes who find happily-ever-
after with three small-town women!

Coming in September 1997—THE PRINCE'S BRIDE

Crown Prince Erik Anders would do anything for his
country—even plan a pretend marriage to his lovely
castle caretaker. But could he convince the king, and
the rest of the world, that his proposal was real—before
his cool heart melted for his small-town "bride"?

Coming in November 1997—THE PRINCE'S BABY

Irresistible Prince Whit Anders was shocked to
discover that the summer romance he'd had years
ago had resulted in a very royal baby! Now that
pretty Drew Davis's secret was out, could her kiss
turn the sexy prince into a full-time dad?

**Look for prince number three in the exciting
conclusion to ROYAL WEDDINGS,
coming in 1998—only from**

▼ *Silhouette* ROMANCE™

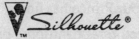
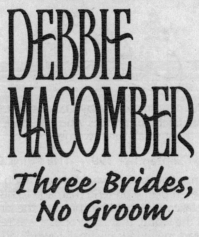